KILLER STRANGELETS

Published in Great Britain by
Inside Pocket Publishing Limited
First published in Great Britain in 2010

Text copyright © C T Furlong, 2009

The right of C T Furlong to be identified as the author of this work has been asserted in accordance with the Copyright, Designs and Patents Act 1988.

All rights reserved. No part of this publication may be reproduced, stored in a retrieval system or transmitted in any form or by any means, electronic, mechanical, photocopying, recording or otherwise, without the prior permission of the publishers.

A CIP catalogue record for this book is available from the British Library

ISBN 978-0-9562315-6-7

Inside Pocket Publishing Limited Reg. No. 06580097
Printed and bound in Great Britain by
CPI Bookmarque Ltd, Croydon

www.insidepocket.co.uk

KILLER STRANGELETS

by C T Furlong

an arctic⁶ adventure

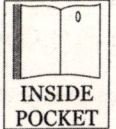
INSIDE POCKET

For Scarlet and Rosanna

Prologue

Slowly, almost imperceptibly, a satellite twenty two thousand miles above the earth rotates. The technician at ground control enters a command into his computer...
Nothing...
He tries again...
Still nothing!
Frustrated, he enters the command for the third time and bashes the return key; still no response. Scratching his head, he consults his emergency manual.

After rifling through several pages, he flicks the book closed, takes off his glasses, and picks up his phone.

Nervously, his finger hovers over the number pad. He almost cannot believe what he is about to say. Then, scratching his head a few more times, he finally accepts that he has no choice. He dials his boss's number.

'Um...sir...we've got a situation here. I've got a rotation and I can't seem to stop it.'

'What do you mean, you can't stop it?' shouts the supervisor angrily.

'Well, we don't seem to be in control of its movements, sir!' replies the man timidly.

'Well, who the hell is then?' barks his superior.

'The signal seems to be coming from everywhere.'
'That's just not possible.'
'I know, sir, but you should see it. It's unbelievable!'

1
The Messenger

We've come so far now - I just can't believe that we're going to fail. But... the truth is... that if you don't help us, then fail we will. And honestly, if you listen to what I have to tell you, failure is so not an option. It's not just my life that's on the line here. It's not just yours, either! I'm not even talking about just saving the planet. I know how completely out-there this sounds, but... well... it's actually the fate of the universe that I'm worried about.

I can imagine how ridiculous this seems. How could I, Iago Johnson, a) know anything about the fate of the universe and, b) be in any kind of position to change it. Let me get some things straight first: I am not a superhero - I'm not a genius - I'm not any braver than the next guy. I'm not even very good at science... although luckily for me, my cousin Renny is pretty handy at all that stuff.

Anyway, here I am, stuck in this computer room. It could be anywhere. You know, semi-dark, stuffy and filled with computer towers, their small lights flashing, sending trivial bits of information to one of their little friends somewhere else on the planet. There can be times though, when those tiny bits of information can change the world. This is one of those times!

Oh, and it's YOUR tiny bit of information that could change the world. YOU could make the difference. YOU could be the saviour of the universe.

I know what you're thinking... no one person can make that much difference. And you'd be right. One person alone cannot help me, but everyone who does is a link in a chain, a mile on a road, a foot on a bridge. That's why I don't just need your help. I need you to pass this message on to your friends, your family, and your neighbours. It has to be the strongest bridge in the world. It will need to be, if it's to save all our lives.

The computer room I find myself in is at CERN, the European Nuclear Research Centre in Switzerland. This place has been around for a long time. I don't know much about what they do here, but here's what I do know... they are trying to create a sort of, mini BIG BANG – you know... the birth of the universe... creation of matter... big, big... well... BANG! They say it will be mini, but no one knows, it could be a very big, BIG BANG...

Here at CERN, they have built a 27 km circular tunnel, running under the Swiss mountains. Those crazy scientists call it the Large Hadron Collider (LHC). Wonder what happened to the small hadron collider? Anyway, it's actually pretty cool when you see it up close. Ginormous magnets, connected together, all perfectly aligned so that protons can be whizzed around it in opposite directions, eventually crashing into each other, causing... you guessed it... a mini BIG BANG.

The problem is that the mini Big Bang is only one of the possible deadly effects of smashing protons together. There are others, maybe not as spectacular and newsworthy, but still deadly, deadly dangerous. Let me tell you what I know!

But first, I need to tell you how I came to know it...

2
The Mistake

It started out like any other Friday. Mum had already drifted in and out of our morning. Dad scurried down the stairs, on his phone, as usual, waving goodbye as he closed the door with his foot. I made sure I had my tennis bag and Aretha picked up her violin case, as we raced after him. Dad was still in the driveway, fumbling in his jacket pocket for his keys.

'Yeah - listen man...,' he was saying to whoever was on the other end of the phone, 'this deal gives you the best of everything... iTunes is here to stay, and a small percentage of something is better than a big percentage of nothing at all!'

'Hmmm! Wise words Dad,' I thought. *'Maybe he's cooler than I give him credit for.'* Dad works for a big music company, hence Aretha's name. And my mum - she runs a theatre company. So you won't be surprised to hear that I'm named after some villain from Shakespeare. S'pose it's better than a nerdy hero's name, though.

'Bye Dad,' said Aretha blowing him a kiss and running to the car where Silke, our exchange student, was just starting the engine. Silke honked the horn twice as she passed Dad and he turned and waved. I can still see his hair blowing and a slow smile on his lips as he waved and turned, slipping into his convertible.

'Buckle up guys,' said Silke, grinning wickedly into the rear-view mirror. Aretha looked at me, a hint of fear in her eyes. When Silke said that, we knew we were in for a rough ride! Silke's dad is some mega-rich Swiss banker that Dad has known for years. To be honest, at first we were dreading meeting her. We thought that anyone that mega rich was bound to be a bit, well... stuck up! But actually, she's cool; we have a lot of fun together. The only thing she really has to do is drop us at school in the morning, and pick us up again in the evening. She usually brings us straight round to Uncle Jonas' and Aunt Meg's after school. Uncle Jonas is Dad's identical twin, but as far as personalities go, theirs couldn't be more different.

We got to school more or less on time. We were late leaving most mornings but then Silke would drive like a lunatic, honking and - I'm guessing here - swearing in German all the way.

Slamming on the brakes at the last minute, Silke stopped just inches behind Uncle Jonas' beaten up old Volvo estate. In the back, their huge golden retriever, Henry, woofed at us, as soon as he dared to lift his head. We couldn't actually hear his 'woof' since all the doors were closed but we could see his mouth opening and closing. His tail was wagging like crazy! He was hoping that this was going to be a fun day out. Poor Henry! Wait 'til he realised that he wasn't coming with us. There'd be disappointed drool all over the boot!

My cousins spilled out of the car - Cam first, then Renny and finally, Tara. Uncle Jonas struggled with his seatbelt. For an incredibly clever man he was so totally useless!

I put my stuff down and went to help him.

'Ah Iago old boy! Thanks a million. I'm really all fingers and thumbs today. It's sooo exciting - you see!'

'See what, Uncle Jonas?'

'Oh, I can't say too much, your father would go crazy,' he started.

'What would Dad possibly have to go crazy about?' I asked, my eyebrows furrowing in confusion. Uncle Jonas took my arm and pulled me alongside him as we walked away from the car and the others. 'Well, you know the book I've been working on!' he grinned. 'Y-yes,' I stammered. He had mentioned it to me several times, but for the life of me, I couldn't remember what it was all about. Something about the universe was all I could remember...*at that time!*

'Well, I told your Dad about it and he said that, although it wasn't his thing, he could pass it on to a few contacts he had in the publishing world.'

'Wow, great news Uncle Jonas! Is someone going to publish your book?' I interrupted. 'No!' he replied with a wink and a grin. 'More incredible than that... someone wants to buy the movie rights!'

'Pheeuuww!' I whistled.

'We're having a "meet" today,' he chuckled. He seemed pleased with himself to be using Dad's lingo.

'So, where's the meet going down?' I teased him. He completely missed my tease. Touching his nose, he winked as he replied, 'Chez Fred, two o'clock, so I've got a bit of time to get ready. Your Dad says I can't go looking like this and I haven't got anything else, so he lent me a suit.' I looked down at his scruffy shorts and sandals and nodded my head. 'I don't always agree with the Gregster but I'm with him this time!' I checked my watch.

'You're in good hands, Uncle Jonas!' I shouted back over my shoulder, running at full speed towards the school doors.

'I know! I know!' he smiled as he got back into the car. I just heard the squeal of his brakes before the school doors closed behind me. Uncle Jonas drove the way he dressed - badly!

3
The Mix-Up

School that day was pretty normal. You know - way too much maths for anyone with a life! I hung around the corridor with Cam and Charlie at break-time. Charlie's well, she's just Charlie – you know... Smart, funny, cool! Charlie and Cam have been friends since as long as they can remember. Charlie loves running. We're both on the athletics team and I've seen her run. She can fly! Sorry, you probably didn't need to know all that, did you?

'So, do you two want to come with me to The Blue-Pool later?' asked Charlie. She's crazy about tropical fish. 'They've got this beautiful new seahorse. It's yellow on the body with blue fins. It costs like a gazillion pounds so I know I'll never have it, but I can dream...'

Cam and I looked at each other and shuffled our feet a bit. Neither of us said a word. We just continued rubbing imaginary specks of dirt from the side of one shoe with the other.

'Oh, I suppose you've got something way more interesting to do... like saving the planet or something,' she joked.

'Just not that into seahorses Charl',' said Cam, slightly nervously.

'It's OK, I understand,' said Charlie sadly, turning her back to us. She began to walk away, slowly.

'OK, I'll come then!' I blurted out. She had only taken three steps but I couldn't stop myself.

'Great!' she grinned, running back and hugging me. I felt a bit embarrassed and, from her reaction, so did she. She sort of, jumped backwards, and smoothed her clothes, self-consciously.

'I suppose I'll come along too then!' said Cam. He knew he didn't really have a choice unless he wanted to hang around with Aretha and Tara.

Renny would be off down by the ditch at the edge of the playing field checking up on his frog-breeding experiment. In the spring, he had taken some dark green frogs from the pond in the woods at the back of their house. He had set them free in the ditch near school, where the frogs were a bit more yellow. He had been monitoring the frogspawn on a daily basis to see if he had created a new hybrid! Renny was definitely like his Dad - a typical science nerd!

* * *

'Where you going?' called Aretha as she spotted us, heading for the main gate after school.

'BluePool,' I replied.

'Can we come too?' she asked, smiling sweetly.

'Don't you and Tara want to hang out with your friends?' I didn't really want them tagging along.

'We promise we'll be really quiet,' whispered Tara cheekily.

'Like two tiny mice, scurrying along behind you,' smiled Aretha.

15

'Alright,' said Cam, making the decision, 'but one peep and you're on your own!'

'Yes Sir, Sir!' said the two girls loudly, saluting Cam as they walked past.

'Someone'd better tell Renny where we're going then,' I said, suddenly remembering him.

'I will,' shouted Charlie over her shoulder, as she sprinted towards the ditch. I held out my phone and was about to say, 'I'll call him,' but then I decided it was much more interesting to watch Charlie run...

* * *

'So Renny, you've decided to come along too,' I teased.

'Research purposes,' he mumbled, looking shyly at Charlie. Charlie smiled and Renny blushed. Then he carried on babbling about genetic characteristics and dominant traits. Charlie didn't seem to mind – she's pretty interested in science too.

We all arrived at The BluePool more or less together.

'Oh Wow!' cooed Tara when Charlie showed her the sea horse.

No matter how much I liked Charlie, I didn't find sea horses that interesting, so I skulked up to the next tank. Renny went somewhere down the back of the shop to check out the ugly fish. Cam and I were soon bored and decided to go and hang about outside the shop, to wait for the others.

As we stood with our hands in our pockets, kicking at pebbles, a pretty ordinary looking silver saloon car sped past us and screeched to a halt outside a restaurant, a bit further up the street.

'Sounds like your dad's driving that,' I laughed.

'Yeah…does!' chuckled Cam, in reply.

'Is that Chez Fred's, or whatever it's called?' I asked, almost to myself.

'No idea,' replied Cam. 'Why?'

'Your Dad told me he had a meeting there today.'

Suddenly we heard shouting coming from the direction of the restaurant. Frowning, I turned away from Cam to see three men jumping out of the car. They raced forward, grabbing some guy who had been sitting on the terrace outside the restaurant and dragged him away. The other people at the table stood up to protest, but something made them sit back down. Cam turned towards me, a frown crossing his face. 'Something's not right here,' he muttered.

'Not much we can do though! Do you think we should call the police?' I said, reaching for my phone. For some reason my hand seemed to be moving in slow motion.

None of the diners moved a muscle while the men ran back to the car with their prisoner. The engine started before the doors closed and the car came screeching back towards where we were standing. Acting on instinct, Cam and I backed towards the shelter of The BluePool's revolving door. Just before we slipped back inside, I caught a glimpse of the "captive" in the back seat. The man with the gun pressed against the side of his head looked very, very familiar.

I shook my head.

It couldn't be.

Then Cam said, 'Was that your dad?'

For some reason the air stopped getting to my lungs…

17

4
The Memory

Cam hit me on the back and I started breathing again. At first, I just stood there, gasping for breath. Finally, in control of my breathing, I lifted my head to face Cam.

'You all right?' he said, as a procession of blurred images passed in front of my eyes.

'I... I... don't know,' I said, wiping my eyes, feeling the blurring caused by welling tears. I felt rooted to the ground. I couldn't imagine what I should do next. I couldn't imagine doing anything at all... actually. I'm not totally sure if Cam sensed my paralysis, but I felt him grabbing me. Before I knew it, I was running alongside my cousin.

As we reached the restaurant, I saw Uncle Jonas sit down heavily and bury his face in his hands. Cam yelled, 'Dad, what in the hell just happened?' Uncle Jonas just sat there shaking his head.

'I... I... don't know,' he replied weakly. 'I just went to the car, to get some papers I'd forgotten and then...' His head slumped forward on to the table.

'Can someone tell us what just happened?' I shouted, looking around the table at the "movie people". It seemed that anger had recovered my lost voice.

'Sit down son,' said one of them gently. 'I'm Artie and

I've known your dad for a long time. This must be some kind of crazy mix-up. I'm sure this will all be sorted out in no time.' He patted my arm, comfortingly. I wanted to scream at this patronising idiot, but Uncle Jonas stood up suddenly.

'No it won't!' his voice quivered, as he tried to control some inner monster. Banging his fists on the table, I saw his face had turned a livid red, between the deep white frown lines.

'This is *all* my fault,' he sniffed. 'I shouldn't have dragged Greg into this. But… how was I to know that this was going to happen? I wish I'd never got involved in that project!'

'What are you talking about, Dad?' asked Cam, a bit calmer now.

Uncle Jonas looked up at him. The anger monster, having reared its head, suddenly disappeared and he whimpered, 'The project at CERN.'

'You mean the LHC experiment?' probed Cam, gently.

'What's the LHC,' I asked.

'The Large Hadron Collider,' answered Cam, turning his face towards me, 'is… well… I think it's better if Dad explains what it is.'

'You remember the project I've been working on at CERN?' Uncle Jonas began.

'Wait, wait,' I said gripping my head in both hands. The thudding seemed quieter like this. 'I… I know you've told me before but… well, I'm finding it hard to just breathe right now. Please remind me exactly what the Large Hadron Collider does. And more importantly, what on earth has it got to do with my dad being kidnapped?'

Uncle Jonas sat up straight and began, 'The LHC is a

giant particle accelerator.'

'Stop, stop!' I yelled. 'What is a particle accelerator?'

'It does what it says on the tin - it accelerates particles!'

I must have looked annoyed at his humour because he frowned apologetically.

'OK,' he continued, 'a particle accelerator sends little pieces of matter, in this case protons, around a very long tunnel, at very high speeds.'

'And, why would you want to do that?' I asked, playing devil's advocate.

'Well... if you send protons spinning around it in opposite directions, you can cause them to crash.' Here, he smashed his fists together, for effect. We all got the picture.

'And, causing protons to crash is exciting because...?' I asked, sarcastically.

'Because, that's what happened at the birth of the universe.'

'The birth of the universe?'

'Yes - just moments after the Big Bang.'

'Wait, let me just get this straight; this LHC is going to recreate the Big Bang?'

'Well, not exactly,' he replied, flustered. 'It will be a sort of, mini Big Bang.'

'You mean... the birth of the universe, but smaller?' I probed. 'Isn't that just a tiny bit dangerous?'

'Well it is, a bit,' he agreed, rubbing his eyes.

A chill ran down my spine.

'There could be some seriously dangerous side effects to crashing protons, like microscopic black holes and matter-annihilating particles.'

'What... exactly... are matter-annihilating particles?' I almost whispered.

Uncle Jonas looked around the table. The movie people nodded. It seemed like everyone wanted him to carry on. Taking a deep breath, he said, 'They destroy matter!'

He let it hang… And it did. Nobody moved, but nervous electricity smouldered in the air.

'For real?' asked a now sweating Artie.

'Everything has been only theoretical up to now. We haven't had any collisions, so we don't know what could happen. But I was worried enough that I designed a fail-safe, a sort of emergency "off-switch". My role in the LHC design was small, but important.' He looked from one to the other of us, checking that we all understood.

'So… my fail-safe can shut down the entire operation!' He furrowed his eyebrows angrily. 'You see I didn't trust all of my colleagues. You know how it is. We were all supposed to be working together, but scientists are very competitive. You don't get a Nobel Prize for just helping someone else to discover something great. No one remembers the name of the scientist who nearly discovered $e=mc^2$. You have to be the first… the One!

'When I worked at CERN, I was worried that there was not enough theoretical research. We were talking about recreating the birth of the universe! A mini Big Bang! We're still not sure if it will actually be mini! He paused for effect, making eye contact with all around the table. Inhaling deeply he carried on, 'I fought my corner for many years and eventually all of my colleagues except one, agreed to slow down the timetable until we were sure of the theory. That's what I have been working on for the last year or so - theoretical modelling of a mini big bang.'

'What does that mean, Uncle Jonas?' I asked.

'It's kind of like a computer simulation. I do thousands

and thousands of imaginary collisions inside my computer, to see what will happen. My colleagues have been working on the other anomalies we might encounter. The mini Big Bang should be the least of our concerns. If there is *an... instability...*'

'You mean... a black hole,' I said.

'Yes, Iago. A black hole.'

'Why don't you call it a black hole, then?'

'Because, it makes people worried. Anyway, if we do see a black hole, it should be so small that it fades away, or collapses almost immediately. The other side effects of our experiments could be more dangerous. And in the wrong hands...'

'How does all this lead to my dad being kidnapped?' I asked, shaking my head.

He closed his eyes in frustration as he battled to control himself. 'One of my colleagues, Katarina Kreng, couldn't accept our terms and quit, promising revenge...' His anger seemed totally spent now and he looked sad and lost.

'We never heard anything more from her. After a while we sort of forgot about her.' He hung his head and began shaking it, muttering, 'But...after what happened this morning, and now this! I'm sure she is up to something!'

'What do you mean "this morning?"' I snapped.

'Iago, I'm sorry. I had no idea that I would drag your father into this. But I should have realised. How could I have missed the connection?'

Uncle Jonas was quiet for a few moments, deep in thought. His eyes were darting back and forth. Clearly, he was trying to put all the pieces together. He took a deep breath...

'It started with a strange phone call yesterday. It was

from my dear old friend Bombay Bob. Bob and I go back a very long way. We met on the first day of term in the Chemistry Lab.' Uncle Jonas smiled wistfully, and then carried on, 'He accidentally spilled hydrochloric acid on my shoe. How we laughed as tiny holes began to appear in my new leather brogues. Then my foot started to feel a bit hot, so I quickly undid my shoe and shook it off. You could see all the way through to the sole. Lucky I hadn't worn my Converses that day or we might not be such good friends. A pair of shoes can be replaced; a foot's a bit trickier! Yeah, me, Bob and Hali O'Gorman did everything together. We even ended up working together!' Uncle Jonas looked off into the distance, reliving old memories.

'And?' I said sarcastically, dragging him back to the present.

'Well...,' he continued, 'One of the reasons I thought the phone call was odd was because it was just that! It was a direct call to my landline. Who uses that kind of method of communication these days? Apart from your grandmother, of course!' He looked at both Cam and I.

'Anyway, Bob said that something had gone wrong with the security systems and that there was a lockout at CERN. When he and all the staff had tried to enter the site, they had been turned away by security and told to go home. Something to do with the security grid not accepting passes. Since it happened to be a Friday, most of them were happy to take the day off and enjoy a long weekend. Bob decided to take his motorbike and go up to Lake Geneva for the weekend. Maybe take the train up the mountainside. He had heard there was a beer brewed up there, which could only be drunk at that altitude. Apparently, if you take it back down the mountain, it goes flat. Something to do with specific gravity, he said. He couldn't get in touch with Ike, Steve, or Gray, the other members of our research team, but he didn't seem that worried. They had all been working quite hard and had probably decided to switch off all communication devices. He had left everything behind, except his laptop and so he was calling from a payphone at a café. He said that he would send an email round when he got up to the lake and that he'd check back regularly. He seemed fine. He said the sun was shining and he was having fun.'

'Dad, that all sounds normal to me. Why do you think that has anything to do with what happened to Uncle Greg?' asked Cam.

'Because of the email'

'What email, Uncle Jonas?'

'Well, this email,' he replied, swivelling his laptop around, so we could all see. The title read, "The Killer Strangelets need you!"

Uncle Jonas continued, 'At first, I thought it was from one of my colleagues, just a silly joke mail, but when I opened it I saw that it was just an invitation to a gig tonight in Geneva. The "Killer Strangelets" are some rock band!'

'OK, I'm still not with you Uncle Jonas. What does this have to do with your work or your colleagues… or my Dad?' I was starting to get a bit snippy.

Uncle Jonas looked at me sadly. 'I'm such a fool, Iago. Killer Strangelets were the side effect of our experiments that most worried me, and Katarina Kreng had an unnatural fascination with them. Killer Strangelets occur when the protons used in the experiment are separated into quarks and gluons. Some of these quarks can become "strange". You don't need to know how this all happens, but if these "strange quarks" become negatively charged they could, in theory, gobble up matter. It would be like a chain reaction. In the blink of an eye, the universe would disappear. I don't think I have to tell you what happens to us! Do I?'

I slumped down into a chair as the shock waves of what Uncle Jonas had explained went through my brain. How could two tiny protons, being smashed together, cause the universe and all life to disappear? I couldn't get my head around it! I could see Cam squeezing his eyes shut, trying to work it out, too. Cam was much better at science than I was, so I was glad to see him struggling.

'OK,' I began. 'I think it's going to take me a while to get my brain to understand all this science but I still have one question… Why on earth did they take my dad?'

'Just a stupid mistake,' replied Uncle Jonas sadly. 'I had forgotten some papers and ran back to the car to get them. When I got here, they were driving off with Greg. They must have had a photo of me. If only Greg and I weren't identical twins!'

'But what does this Kreng woman want with you?'

'I'm guessing that she just wants me out of the picture. I'm the only one who knows where the fail-safe is and how to arm it. The truth is… if I'm not around, she can potentially… well… end life as we know it…'

5
The Milkshake

'*Um... Hellooo! Iago! It's me. Can you see me?*'

'*Sorry, it's Aretha. Just got to check on how they're doing. Won't take a minute...*'

'*Hey little sis', how are you? Where's Tara? I can't see her.*'

'*She's OK. She's just behind me. Why did we have to get the crummiest job, Iago?*'

'*Don't moan, Aretha. Remember what Charlie's going through right now!*'

'*OK, OK, I suppose I am feeling a bit sorry for myself. It's just that we have been hanging around here forever. I don't know if I can drink another milk-shake ever again.*'

'*Aretha, if I could think of another way – I would. You have to wait until you get the go ahead from Renny. Your job might be boring and very hard but it's absolutely critical. If we can't get the message out, we will fail! And failure's not an option. There won't be a second chance...*'

'*Yeah...I know. Aretha, over and out... Oh, wait. Tara wants to have a word.*'

'*Hey Iago!*'

'*Is that a human being or a strawberry milk-shake? Oh, wait - it's Tara!*'

'Don't laugh at me, Iago! You'll regret it later! You know what I saw last night. It only takes one small slip of the tongue and she knows!'

'Just you dare, Tara. I swear, I'll...Oh I can't think of what right now but I've got time on my hands! Anyway, what did you want to say?'

'Oh yeah - any word from Cam recently?'

'No, nor Renny. But I'm sure I'll hear any minute now. I'll let you know as soon as I do.'

'Hope they're doing OK.'

Yeah! Me too, Tar'...'

'Talk later!'

'OK. Be patient and keep an eye on Aretha. She seems down.'

'Will do, Cuz. Tara, over and out!'

6
The Missing

'So! Some mad woman, intent on destroying the universe, has taken my dad?' I stammered. I felt deeply sad now, and a horrible feeling of terror swept over me. I wanted to scream, like a child. I needed help, but the one person I could usually count on was not able to help me. He was the one who needed help now.

'Well... what are we going to do to get him back, Dad?' asked Cam, who by now was pacing up and down agitatedly. Uncle Jonas frowned. 'I don't know what the right thing to do is. If I don't give myself up who knows what she'll do to him. But if I do...' He put his head in his hands.

'The fail-safe override thing; they will get it out of you eventually,' Cam said, quietly.

'They'll torture Dad or use him to get to you.' This was a no win situation. My pain was turning to anger now.

'Without doubt we've been dealt a rotten hand,' said Uncle Jonas sagging.

I didn't respond for a few seconds; an idea was ping-ponging around in my head.

'Then we don't play this hand!' I said defiantly, enjoying my poker reference.

'What hand do we play, then?' asked Cam, sarcastically.

'We come up with a plan of our own. We take it to them. We force their hand.' I was feeling very brave now. I didn't know how we were going to do it but we were going to stop these people and rescue my father.

Then my well-laid plans went awry! Out of nowhere, some men in suits and sunglasses arrived. Most of them were big and burly. They all had earpieces and I suspected that they were some kind of "secret service" agents. Though they looked like some middle-aged boy band revival troupe! I sniggered out loud. The brain does some funny things in moments of total stress!

'Come with us, Mr Johnson,' said one of them dragging Uncle Jonas to his feet. Then they dragged the "movie people" to their feet as well.

'Hey sonny, what the heck do you think you're doing?' shouted Artie. 'Do you know who I am?' The lead agent stepped up to Artie and raised his glasses. 'Yes, Mr Magill. We know you very, very well!' Artie's eyebrows flew up. He was clearly shocked.

'We've long suspected this fool was into something dangerous,' he sneered at Uncle Jonas. 'We've been watching and listening.' He pointed off into the distance. I followed his gaze but I couldn't see anyone listening. I supposed he meant they had some kind of electronic eavesdropping equipment somewhere over there. 'Now you all better come with us. We've got a few questions that need answering.' With that, he bent down and grabbed Artie roughly. 'Are you outta your mind?' screamed Artie. 'I'm a movie producer! I'm not a terrorist! You can't take me…'

'We'll see about that,' laughed the agent, as his colleague

started dragging the others away.

'Uncle Jonas…' I half whispered. Then the lightning bolt struck my brain and terror froze my limbs. I realised that without Uncle Jonas there was no way on earth we would ever find my dad.

7
The Mumble

'*Hsssssss... Not sure where... heading south... think!'*
'Hang on... I think that might be Cam!'
'Cam, Cam - Is that you? I can't see anything. Just some blurred lines and a lot of out of focus objects.'
....
'...hear something...be talking...ask...'
'Cam, are you running? Stop running, for heaven's sake!'
'Hhsssssss'
....
'Please try again Cam...'
Nothing...

8
The Mission

As the secret service dragged Uncle Jonas and the others away for questioning, Renny came running towards us. Never surprised by anything, he just coolly asked, 'What's going on with Dad then?'

'Jeez Renny, show some emotion. Dad's being dragged off by some kind of secret service agents and Uncle Greg's been kidnapped!' Cam said, his voice quivering with frustration.

'Hey, don't take it out on me,' said Renny defensively.

'He's right Cam,' I said, taking his elbow, 'it's not his fault!' Then, totally out of character Renny ran towards his father shouting, 'Daaad – don't let them take you too!' Cam and I looked at each other, confused.

It was true that Renny and his dad shared some kind of scientific bond but well, like I said Renny didn't show emotion. Not even when one of his pets died. And he had buried many. He said that he saw the "bigger picture" of life and that you couldn't feel sad about every creature that came to an untimely end.

Uncle Jonas turned back towards his son. Renny threw his arms around his father's neck. Their heads were almost locked together with Uncle Jonas's on the outside, away from the agent, who was holding his arm. I noticed that Uncle Jonas's lips were moving. He was whispering something to Renny.

Finally, Renny unlocked his arms and the agent dragged Uncle Jonas away from him. Tears were rolling down Renny's face as he turned back towards us. As soon as his back was to the agents, he grinned wickedly and winked at Cam and I. It was all we could do to keep straight faces. Renny was such a ham actor!

He sidled up to us and mumbled coolly, 'Walk with me guys!'

We followed him back to The BluePool, where the girls were just coming out through the revolving doors. Charlie, who had been laughing, stopped suddenly, a frown crossing her brow when she saw my face. Her eyes searched mine. It was as if she were trying to read me.

'Follow us!' I hissed at them as I passed.

'Iago, I don't think I like your tone,' she huffed. I walked back and grabbing her by the arm, I looked down into her bright blue eyes.

'Please Charlie, no games. Just this once - follow me!'

'What is it?' she asked. Now she could see the fear and anger in my eyes. She knew I was serious.

'Not in front of the others,' I said, looking towards Aretha and Tara.

'Come on ladies,' she said and she smiled sweetly back over her shoulder at the girls.

Turning on her heel, she grabbed my arm, dragging me forward.

'What's going on?' she hissed.

'Dad's been kidnapped and Uncle Jonas has been taken away by MI5 or MI6 or something. That just sounds so

33

ridiculous when I say it - I won't blame you if you don't believe me.'

'Iago, you're scaring me. You're like some bumbling old fool. You're not making any sense.' Charlie stepped back and stared at me.

My head drooped and for the first time that day, I felt like a child. Charlie could do that to me. She could see through me. In her eyes, I could see the person I really was, not the person I was pretending to be. She knew me somehow. I don't mean she knew what my favourite song was or how many times I hit snooze on my alarm clock in the morning (at least four FYI) but she knew me on the inside. Sometimes that scared me!

Cam interrupted, 'For heaven's sake, we'll never get anywhere if you two keep staring into each other's eyes.' He looked a bit peeved. I knew why! He liked Charlie - a lot!

'Cam, you insensitive yeti!' snarled Charlie. Her eyes flashed angrily and she turned her face away from him with a 'hmmmphhh!'

Renny started to speak quietly. At first, we almost didn't pay attention to him. He tended to babble a bit and we were used to his ramblings. This time though, something was different. He just kept repeating the same series of colours 'blue, green, blue, blue, green, orange, white, black, black, brown, red.'

'Renny are you all right?' laughed Tara. She frowned as she studied her brother.

'Even for Renny, this is weird!' she said, sighing. Even though she didn't know what was going on, she sensed the atmosphere. None of us was in the mood for one of Renny's jokes.

Aretha walked up to Renny and began to stroke his arm tenderly. Like I said, Aretha is a sweetie. She just is! She is always concerned about other people and her gentleness works on everyone, even Renny. 'Rens,' she started softly 'are you upset? Is that why you keep repeating the colours? Does it comfort you?'

'PEN,' shouted Renny between 'green' and 'orange'. He carried on repeating the colour sequence. Aretha jumped back, surprised. She fumbled in her bag and found her pen. It was luminous pink with feathers at the top.

'Sorry, it's all I've got,' she apologised, passing it to Renny.

He raised his eyebrows crossly as he took the pen, still reciting his colour sequence like a mantra. Then he began to mime drawing movements in the air.

Aretha looked back confused. 'Oh, paper!' she said, as the penny dropped. She pulled out the paper and Renny grabbed it from her hand.

'Renny!' she cried, 'there's no need to be rude.'

'Sorry Cuz,' Renny smiled as he wrote down the last colour. Then, he turned to look at us. We were all silent. Renny grinned. This was the first time ever, in his life that he was totally in control. He had all our attention and he crossed his arms, savouring the moment. A little too long, as it happened!

Cam launched himself angrily towards Renny. He would have knocked him to the ground, if I hadn't pulled him back. I held onto him while he snarled at Renny. Renny looked at his older brother. He knew how much he annoyed Cam. He knew his moment was over!

'Alright, alright!' he began 'the colour code is the key to Dad's fail-safe mechanism.'

'What on earth are we supposed to do with that information?' asked Charlie, confused. I looked around at the faces of my cousins and my friend.

Silence!

I stared at Cam. He nodded his head. I couldn't bring myself to say it - it seemed ridiculous. No, I wasn't going to even suggest it. Then I looked at Aretha. In her scared, confused eyes, I saw my dad. From somewhere down deep in my stomach, a seed of courage fought its way out.

'We're going to… help my Dad!' I said, sounding braver than I felt.

'Whoo-hoo!' shouted Renny as he punched the air.

'ARCTIC 6 - on a mission!'

Neither of us had any idea what Renny was on about, but then no one ever did!

9
The Misgivings

The bus journey back to Uncle Jonas' house seemed to take forever. Nobody spoke one word, not while we waited at the bus stop, nor on the bus. Charlie sat opposite me, just staring at me. I found it quite hard to concentrate, to be honest. Charlie's stare is intense. My mind was a blur of flashing images and useless thoughts. I had an annoying nursery rhyme going round in my head. Why do they always strike at moments like that? Do they lurk around, just waiting to pounce?

Cam sat at the back of the bus, alone. I guessed that he was getting in a bit more "thinking" than I was. I turned my head to look at him a couple of times. He looked angry and moody. Was it just the situation or was he angry with me? I couldn't really think what I had done to make him angry. I was three months older than he was and so everyone looked to me for leadership. I could run a bit faster than he could but he was better at most ball sports than I was. It's true that he was always the deeper thinker. Did he feel that this made him more qualified to lead our "gang"? I let the question run around in my brain for a while. Then I decided, 'intelligence does not always the best leader make'. I don't know if

I had heard that from some history lesson, but it seemed sensible. Sometimes leaders had to act fast without much time for deep reflection. Sometimes you had to go with your heart, not with your head. And anyway, it was my Dad we needed to rescue. My lip curled in a slight snarl. I was ready to defend my leadership! I was...

Cam tapped me on the shoulder as he passed. We were almost at the stop. 'Drat - not exactly showing leadership there Iago,' I hissed, under my breath. 'Couldn't even stay focussed long enough to be the first off the bus!' Cam jumped down first, with Aretha and Tara following. Grabbing Charlie's arm as he passed her, Renny began whispering conspiratorially. They both got off together leaving me standing on the step.

'Thanks,' I mumbled to the driver as I stepped down. They were all ahead of me walking down the drive.

'Great skill - leading from the rear!' I muttered to myself sarcastically.

'Maybe I shouldn't be the one leading this gang.

10
The Make Up

Still anxious about my ability even to lead a line of ants to a lollipop, I pushed open the front door. Charlie was standing in the hall surrounded by a pile of bags, coats, and shoes and I could hear the sound of raised voices in the kitchen.

'God, I'm getting really tired of all this brooding!' she hissed at me, turning her head to stare angrily at Cam. I could see him, sitting on the couch just inside the living room with his jacket still on and his shoes up on the coffee table. His look definitely said 'stay away'.

I looked at Charlie and shrugged. I couldn't deal with this right now. My dad needed everyone working together. Suddenly, I was terrified I was going to cry. I kind of wanted to. In some weird way, I wanted Charlie to run over and comfort me. But then again, I'd be embarrassed for the rest of my life. She would probably laugh at me! She'd never look at me again.

Auntie Meg ran into the hall with a ball of dough still in her hand. She had been making pizza. Oh, how much did I love Auntie Meg's pizzas? I almost cheered up. Cam had phoned his mother on the way home to explain the situation. Then a wave of panic struck me. 'Mum!' I gasped. I hadn't even thought of calling her. Although she wouldn't be able to do much, she should at least know what had happened to her husband. 'She's on her way over,' smiled Auntie Meg. Maybe it was just the flour on her face but she seemed very pale.

'Charlie,' she whispered, 'would you be a sweetheart and look after the girls for a few minutes. I think I need to speak to my men for a moment.'

She handed Charlie the ball of dough, which Charlie accepted gingerly. She put her floury hand on my shoulder and steered me into the living room, gently closing the door behind us. She sat beside me on the couch, opposite Cam.

'What's up sweetheart?' she said softly to Cam. Cam raising his eyes looked at his mother's face. 'Nothing!' he mumbled. The he shot a glance in my direction.

'If it's about being in charge, I was thinking…,' I began. He cut me off.

'Don't be stupid Iago. They all look up to you.'

'Well what then?' My voice came out a bit higher than I would have liked.

'Cameron,' said his mum, 'tell Iago what's bothering you!'

Cam hesitated. His mouth moved to open, and then he shut it again. He finally muttered, 'I see the way she looks at you. I know it's stupid but I just get angry, that's all!'

'Don't be ridiculous Cam. It's not like that. We're just friends. She doesn't look at me like that. And anyway, I'm not interested!' I was sure I was telling the truth but somehow I felt like I was betraying Charlie.

'Anyway, right now we need to be focussing on something else!' I carried on, a bit more sternly. Why did he have to pick now to have this discussion?

'Boys,' interrupted Auntie Meg, 'I really need to know what happened today. So far, I have had no communication from anyone - police or kidnappers. Your mum,' she said looking at me, 'has had a call from the police. I told her you were there when it happened, so she wants to make sure you're OK before she goes to see them. Like I said she's on her way right now.

11
The Melt Down

Mum arrived with a squeal of brakes and a waft of perfume. She always made dramatic entrances. I think she spent way too much time with actors! Of course, she was wearing her Bluetooth earpiece and waffling to someone on the other end. Racing up to me, she threw her arms around me, kissing me on the head, never missing a word of her phone conversation. She looked around for Aretha, who came running out of the kitchen and threw her arms around her mummy. Aretha began to sob now. I was a bit shocked. I felt bad that I hadn't been thinking about my little sister. She was going through this too and she clearly needed someone to comfort her. I vowed to make sure I paid more attention to her feelings in future. She was my responsibility now!

'Meg!' said Mum loudly, finally pulling the earpiece out. 'What on earth is going on? The police, or whoever they are, say that Greg's been kidnapped. It just seems so hard to believe?' Throwing herself down on the couch, she let out a huge sigh. Aretha snuggled up beside her. My mum stroked her hair, putting some loose strands behind her ear.

Auntie Meg shuffled a bit nervously. Mum always

had this effect on her. Taking a deep breath and looking in my direction she said, 'I think the kids should explain, Marguerite!'

'Mum,' I started. 'What Auntie Meg told you is true. Dad's been kidnapped and some "agents" have taken Uncle Jonas. They seem to have got the impression that Dad was selling Uncle Jonas' "work" to some bad guys.'

'What work?' she asked. I could tell she was getting bored so I decided to speed things up. Straight, and to the point, worked best with Mum.

'Work that, in the wrong hands, could kill us all and annihilate the entire universe!' That got her attention. She sat bolt upright and looked at Auntie Meg.

Auntie Meg steeled herself and said, 'It's true!'

'WHHAAAATTT?' screamed Mum.

We all remained completely silent.

'I'll get to the bottom of this,' she hissed, in full acting mode now, pushing herself up from the couch. She swung around as she reached the door, her long hair swirling over her shoulder. 'They won't know what hit them!' With that, she sashayed out the door.

Sometimes, I had to love my mum. I knew that those "agents" would live to regret this day. When she came at you, all guns blazing, there was nothing scarier.

12
The Madness

As usual, the quiet she left behind affected us all. She was such a strong person. To be honest, we all felt a bit weaker now she'd gone. At least I know I did. Walking back into the room, Charlie turned to me. I looked down. I dared not look at her now. I was terrified of what Cam might read into it.

'Uuuggghh!' screamed Charlie, stamping her foot, exasperated. 'Will someone please tell me what's going on here?'

Auntie Meg smiled saying, 'Only a girl as lovely as you would ask that.'

Charlie's eyes flashed angrily. 'BOYS!' she spat out angrily, as if it were a swear word. And pulling my sleeve, she dragged me over to where Cam stood.

'Right, you two,' she began. She was on fire now! 'Enough of this rubbish today. I'm not remotely interested in either of you, and in fact…' She was screaming now, 'I don't even want to be friends with you when this is over…'

'Ehem…?' coughed Renny. All three of us turned to glare at him. Poor Renny! Six virtual laser targets lit up his body. If we had had weapons, Renny would have been toast.

'Look, I know you all think I'm a geek, or a nerd, or whatever!' he looked at us accusingly. No one flinched. 'Anyway, the point is that, I sometimes assist Dad with his research and stuff.' He looked around smugly. 'So I know a bit about his project. Like I said earlier, I even know a bit about the "fail-safe."' He waited to see how we would respond - no one batted an eyelid. He stared like a rabbit in the headlights.

'Well,' he continued, his voice beginning to shake a little. 'I've been thinking, and I think I know how we can help your dad... I mean... we'll have to work out a detailed plan, but I think I can help with the science part.'

'What science part?' asked Tara, peeking round the door. She and Aretha had clearly been eavesdropping.

'Yeah, what science part?' asked Cam, sarcastically.

'Well I can work out what we need to do when we get to CERN,' replied Renny, matter-of-factly.

'When we get to CERN...?' we all chorused, in amazement.

13
The Mum Problem

'Renny, you know I love you son, but that's absolutely ridiculous! said Auntie Meg, standing with her flour-caked hands on her hips. 'Never mind what on earth can a few kids do against violent henchmen, who can kidnap a man in broad daylight... but CERN is in Switzerland! How on earth do you think you are going to get to Switzerland?' She was quite cross. I had never seen her cross before. Renny slumped down into the armchair, easily defeated by Mum logic.

My mind, however, was racing. Renny's "crazy" idea rolled around my head. Maybe there was something we could do. Desperate times needed desperadoes! I was willing to give anything a shot. I wasn't sure if the others would come along with me but... at least I knew I could count on Renny. But I couldn't let Auntie Meg know that...

'Yeah Renny! Maybe we should just let the adults deal with this situation,' I said, trying my best to sound as if I wasn't interested. Flopping down on the couch next to Cam, I picked up the TV remote. I started mindlessly flicking through channels, as I often did.

'Gimme that,' snapped Cam, grabbing the remote from my hand. Finding some music show, he threw the remote out of my reach.

'I'm not watching this,' said Tara, turning on her heel. 'You coming Aretha?'

Aretha stepped in behind her. She would have gone anywhere with her older cousin. I knew that I would have to work on Tara if I wanted her to come along. The only trouble was that I didn't want Aretha in any danger. Charlie and Tara could take care of themselves, but Aretha was, and maybe would always be, the baby of the gang.

'I think I'm out!' said Charlie, heading for the door. This was her way of saying that she was bored. I couldn't let her leave, not yet. She was a big part of my plan, or at least she would be, when I had time to plan my plan.

'Don't go Charl',' I said standing up suddenly. 'We need to talk!' I looked purposefully at Auntie Meg, raising my eyebrows.

'Em...I've got to go make a couple of phone calls,' said Auntie Meg, excusing herself.

Cam gave me the evil eye. I waited until I heard Auntie Meg's footsteps going into the kitchen before I turned to him.

'Cam, you can drop the deathstare. I'm not going to kiss Charlie in front of you or something.'

'Not ever!' said Charlie, laughing at me. I felt a bit hurt. She didn't have to sound quite so repulsed by me! I let a couple of seconds pass to compose myself.

Then I began...

47

14
The Mindworks

'Renny, your idea is more than just a bit mad, but I think with a bit of work, we might be able to do something.'

'You do?' said Renny, surprised.

'Iago, have you lost your mind?' asked Charlie, astonished.

Cam turned to me. He was still peeved with me. I could tell. Were we never going to get past this? 'What's your brilliant plan then, Iago?' he muttered.

'Listen Cam,' I said. I was getting a bit tired of being the peacemaker. I had done nothing wrong. But I did need him. My Dad needed all of us "with our noses pointing in the same direction," as he would say.

I tried again, 'I don't have everything worked out yet. In fact, I haven't had time to work anything out at all. But, I thought we could come up with something together - the four of us?' I looked from Cam to Charlie.

Charlie sat down beside Cam and looking into his eyes, she said seriously, 'Cam, I don't know what's going on here, but Iago needs our help. Let's put all this to one side for now and just focus?' Cam squirmed about a bit on the couch before finally muttering, 'OK!'

'Good!' said Charlie, standing up. She was running the

meeting now. I didn't mind this - she was a good organiser. She could weigh things up quickly and always noticed the weak spot in an idea or plan. That's not to say that she was negative; she was often the one who came up with the solution in the end.

'Renny, you have the floor!' She mock-bowed at Renny.

'Thank you Madam Speaker,' said Renny seriously, as he stood up and coughed. Even Cam laughed at this!

'Sit down you fool!' I said, laughing.

'Right, where do I begin?' asked Renny. Then he answered his own question. 'Dad's project! Well Dad's project was to design the "alignment" system for the magnets, so that the protons could be directed with precision.'

Charlie piped up sheepishly, 'Um, I think I might have missed something?'

'Oh no, not back to the beginning again,' said Renny, shaking his head while letting it drop to his chest. He pressed his hands to his forehead. 'OK... who knows what the LHC does?' Charlie raised her hand, sheepishly.

'Yes Charlie!' said Renny smugly, like a teacher.

'Well, as far as I know they are going to create a mini big-bang,' she looked at Renny hopefully.

'Well done Charlie. That's one of the experiments they are carrying out,' smiled Renny. He was really overdoing it now.

'Get on with it!' hissed Cam.

'OK, well you know that they will send protons around the tunnel, causing them to crash into each other. They need to direct these protons into each other's path. They do this by using some mega-magnets. And Dad designed the magnet's alignment system! Like Dad said, this is dangerous science and he didn't trust everyone so, into this system, he built a fail-safe mechanism.' He paused here, to check if we were all following.

'Ok… magnets, directing protons,' I summarised. The others nodded.

'We got it,' I answered, for everyone.

'If the fail-safe is triggered, the magnets will NOT align properly and the system will shut down. Then there will be no big-bang or killer strangelets!' He waited while the information sank in. 'What's a killer strangelet?' asked Charlie, looking from Cam to me. She lifted her arms in a shrug, saying, 'What, so everyone here knows what a killer strangelet is?'

'It's an anomaly that could gobble up matter. It could destroy the universe,' I said quietly.

'Oh, this should be a piece of cake then!' said Charlie. She was glaring evilly now and the sarcasm dripped off her tongue. 'We just have to somehow get to Switzerland, somehow get into CERN, somehow find this fail-safe, somehow find your Dad, somehow beat the baddies and somehow save the universe!' She was shouting quite loudly by the end and Cam, Renny and I all tried to squirm as deep into our seats as we could.

15
The Maybe

'OK Charlie,' I began, after she had sat down and I thought she was looking a bit calmer, 'there are definitely a few hurdles we need to jump!' As soon as it came out, I knew that it was a stupid analogy - I was going to pay for that. I winced, waiting for Charlie's cruel tongued reply. And it came...

'This isn't some stupid horse race, Iago.' Oh hell, she was standing up again!

'I mean, I can't even believe we are discussing this,' she continued. 'A bunch of idiots like us are going to pull off something like this?'

'Hey, watch who you're calling an idiot,' said Renny, stupidly. He had a lot to learn about girls, especially girls like Charlie!

She just turned and hissed at him. He shrank back and covered his mouth with his hand.

I tried again, 'Well, I think I might have an idea how we can solve the first problem.' I waited for a response.

'How to get to Switzerland?' asked Cam, although he didn't sound that interested.

'Exactly - my friend!' I replied. I was getting quite excited now. 'We all know that Silke's Dad is mega rich;

so mega rich that he owns his own plane! I'm not saying it's a done deal but we could ask!'

'OK,' said Charlie, 'supposing your plan works. What next?'

I had to admit I was a bit stumped.

'Dad has plenty of schematics of the tunnel,' Renny piped up.

'Good,' said Charlie, back in control again. 'We need to find a way in! Cam, can you do some web research. Maybe there's something we can use?'

'Alright,' said Cam, again not exactly enthusiastically!

'Renny, you need to go over your Dad's work really carefully. It's all very well us getting there and finding the fail-safe. We need to know how to activate it.'

'Iago, you get on the phone to Silke right now. We don't have a moment to loose.' She paced up and down. 'I'll go and tell the girls.' Taking a leaf out of my mother's book, she swept out of the room.

52

16
The Minor Lie

'I'll come right away,' said Silke, as soon as I told her what had happened. I had to admit I felt a bit nervous asking her if we could somehow "borrow" her father's plane. I had worked myself into a bit of a sweat by the time she arrived.

As usual, Silke sped down the drive and slammed on her brakes at the last minute. Jumping out, she ran to Aretha, who was waiting by the door. She swept her up saying, 'Oh you poor baby!' Then she grabbed my arm.

'Iago, I'm so sorry. What can I do to help?'

I was just about to explain, when Auntie Meg came out of the kitchen.

'I thought it was you I heard!' she said smiling. It was hard to mistake Silke's entrance. 'I'm glad you're here, actually.' She led Silke away from us. I could make out the first few words… 'Marguerite just called. I need to go and help them with their…'

I'm pretty sure the last word was "enquiries."

* * *

'Be good!' said Auntie Meg sternly as she walked out the door. 'And do what Silke tells you to.' All six faces smiled back sweetly at her.

'We will,' I said, speaking for everyone. As soon as she got into her car, I ushered everyone inside and closed the door. Tara started jumping up and down with excitement. 'I can't believe we're going to do this!' she said.

'Tara, we don't know if we are going to do anything yet! And even if we do, we've got a hell of a lot of planning to do first!' I replied seriously, turning to Silke.

'We need your help.'

'In vat vay?' she asked, in her heavily accented English.

I explained the situation and our solution to it, very quickly. Her blue eyes never left my face as I talked. I was starting to feel a bit foolish for asking, but I had no choice. 'So, we need to get to Switzerland. Can you help?' I heard myself finish.

Silke was quiet for a moment. Oh no! All our plans were ruined if she wouldn't help us. My heart started to pound very loudly in my ears. I was sure the others could hear it. I looked around at their faces. They didn't seem to hear it! They were all staring at Silke. I looked at her, her mouth was moving but very, very slowly and I could hear a droning sound.

Suddenly, I felt the wall hit me in the back. Weird - that wasn't meant to happen! Silke turned to look at me. Her worried eyes searched my face. Then I heard her voice, 'Are you OK, Iago? You look terrible. Here zit down.' She pushed me back into a chair.

'I zink it must be ze stress!' she said. 'Somebody get vater!' Cam ran to the kitchen.

'I'm fine, I'm fine!' I said, as he came back with the water. 'What were you saying Silke?'

'I vas saying zat I can tell my Dad zat I am homesick.

He vill send ze plane straight away. But zere is a problem - how to get ze six of you on board? Ze pilot vill never agree to become involved.' I thought about it for a while. We would have to take some chances if we were to pull this off!

'We arrange for the plane to come tonight! You can ask the pilot to use the airstrip at Ashfield. It's really dark there. All you need to do is distract the pilot long enough so we can sneak aboard!' I said feeling much better now.

'Yes, I zink zat could vork,' smiled Silke 'but, I vant you to rest a little. Zis has been a crazy day already. Just take it easy. I vill go and call my Father!'

As soon as she left the room, Charlie came over to me. She looked at me, curiously.

'Are you OK?' She looked concerned. For some reason that made me feel warm and cosy.

'He's fine,' said Aretha throwing her arms around my neck. 'He still gets car sick! He's a delicate boy, our Iago!' She laughed and nuzzled her nose against my neck.

'Thanks sis! Really doing wonders for my reputation here!' I replied.

'Well, it's true!' she answered, grinning.

17
The Minutes Tick

We didn't have much time to prepare since Silke returned no more than three minutes later, giving us the thumbs up. I shook my head - as simple as that! We were really, actually going! We didn't have time to prepare anything. We would just have to figure this out as we went along.

'Listen up everyone,' I began, 'we have no idea what we are heading into tonight. You are responsible for your own supplies. Just remember that it's September so it can get pretty cold at night. Bring your warmest coat. Make sure you are wearing jeans. Bring extra socks, and need I say it, underwear! If you have any sweets, chocolate or biscuits stashed away then get them out. Try to keep your backpack small. Remember we will need to do some travelling on foot when we get to Switzerland.'

'Whoo-hoo!' chirped Aretha and Tara, hugging each other and dancing around in circles. I actually think they were more excited than the rest of us. I suppose that sometimes being the youngest is fun! 'Nice to see you're enjoying this, girls,' I scolded.

'Sorry,' replied Tara, reprimanded.

Silke took Aretha and I home to collect our things. I felt

a bit guilty sneaking into our house and secretly preparing my bag. But then I remembered that it was my dad that I was trying to help. Mum would be pretty angry when we got back…When we got back; that made me nervous. I began to wonder if I should have left Aretha out of this. But I knew I couldn't; she was one of us. She had a right to be with us. Together, she and Tara could be really useful, and we needed all hands on board for this one!

I packed my compass and tore the maps of France and Switzerland out of Dad's European road atlas. I was sure he'd forgive me if we rescued him. I found a triple pack of tic-tac in my locker. After several minutes of rummaging, I found my striped wool hat and gloves. I felt a bit silly packing them but considering what we were doing, they might come in handy. Stuffing extra socks and underwear in my bag, I raced downstairs. Silke and Aretha were already in the kitchen checking out the biscuit situation. The biscuit situation was always good in our house, so we had to choose. We decided to go for some muesli bars – for energy! Chocolate digestives – everyone likes them, and six giant chocolate bars – as a last resort! Although Aretha - a real salt addict, wanted to take some crisps, I discouraged her. 'Aretha, can you imagine if we fail at the first hurdle because of your noisy crisp packets! It's already going to be difficult enough trying to sneak six of us on board that plane.' She got the point and decided to eat two packets of crisps there and then just to keep her salt levels up.

'You guys ready?' I shouted, standing by the open front door. The adrenaline was racing through my veins now and I wanted to get going. Finally, the two girls rushed down the hall. Although it didn't matter what Silke was bringing since she was leaving us as soon as we landed, she had still packed a rucksack. I raised my eyebrow, questioning her.

'You never know, you might need me!' she smiled back.

I had to admit that that made me feel less nervous. 'OK, let's go', I said, as macho as I could. The girls looked at each other and grinned. They thought I was funny; that really made me feel cool - not!

Arriving at Cam's house ten minutes later, Silke kept the engine running, while I ran indoors to scare up the others. Cam and Tara were waiting in the hall with their bags packed. Tara's lazy smile told me that she had won the race to pack her bags! Cam looked miserable again; surely not just because Tara had beaten him in some silly race?

'What's up Cam?' I asked, nervously.

'Charlie just called. She might be a non-starter,' he replied glumly.

'What?' I asked - my heart pounding. I really couldn't imagine doing this without Charlie.

'She said her Mum was going to call here. So I guess we're scuppered.' I was silent for a minute, really trying to think of how we could make this happen. Then it came to me! Racing out of the house, I dragged Silke out of the car. I explained my plan to her on the way back inside. As soon as we reached the hall, the phone rang. Cam reached for it. 'No!' I shouted, and then smiled in Silke's direction. Taking her cue, Silke walked to the phone and lifted it to her ear.

'Oh Hello, Mrs Patterson. Yes. Zis iz Silke. Yes - lucky me; I am looking after the whole "gang" zis veekend. Meg and Marguerite have gone for a health veekend. Oh, abzolutely no problem if Charlie stays - ze girls vill be pleased. Yes I absolutely promise zat I vill take good care of zem all! Bye, Mrs Patterson.' She hung up and turned to face us. She looked really serious now and we all felt nervous.

'Zat's it, I come vith you! I am responsible for all of you now and if I zink it's too dangerous zen ve call it off!' She was quite scary now. I was beginning to wonder if we should have left her out of it... Too late now!

Charlie's mum dropped her off and Silke ran out to the car to speak to her. The rest of us stayed behind the blinds - spying. Renny, who was balancing on the back of the couch on his belly, almost gave us away. He wobbled and stayed suspended mid-fall for a few seconds, his head nearly touching the blinds. Luckily, Cam was able to grab his legs to steady him.

'Idiot!' hissed Cam.

After that, Renny decided to lie perfectly still until after Mrs Patterson's car had disappeared down the drive. Charlie raced in, flinging her backpack on the floor.

'Phew, for a terrible half-hour I thought I was going to miss this,' she said and a light shone behind her eyes. 'Thanks Silke,' she said throwing her arms around her.

'OK, everyone in ze car,' ordered Silke. We didn't dare to argue. She might pull the whole operation if we did.

On the way to the airfield, we did some check listing; not that we could go back and get anything we'd forgotten. It was still comforting though, going through everything. Maps? Check! Compass? Check! Torches? Check! Food? Check! Socks and underwear? Check! Toothpaste? No answer. We all looked at each other. Finally Aretha piped up, 'Well you didn't mention it Iago.'

'Don't worry, zere is usually some in ze little bathroom

on ze plane,' Silke said into her rear-view mirror.

'Phew,' said Charlie. 'I couldn't stand my own breath after a weekend of no brushing, never mind any of yours.' We all laughed and suddenly all of us, including Cam, were excited about our adventure.

Whatever Renny called us - we were on a mission!

18
The Midnight Flit

We arrived at the tiny airfield just before dark. Since it was a private airstrip and everything had been arranged by Silke's father and his pilot, we just parked by the empty hangar. Piling out, we all busied ourselves with sorting out our kit. Cam and I scouted around the back of the hangar, to find a place we could hide out once the plane arrived. The others were sitting on the dusty edge of the runway beside the pile of rucksacks waiting for us, when we got back.

'We should try to be over there in the heather, just past the hangar,' I said, pointing. 'I'm guessing that the plane will taxi up to here?' I looked to Silke.

'Yes, he vill assume zat I am vaiting in ze car. I vill call him and ask him to come and valk me to ze plane. Hopefully he vill leave ze door open. Zat is ven you must board!' she replied.

It all seemed to be so simple; everything was going well. That made me really nervous. This was all too easy.

Dusk arrived with a few flecks of orange brightening the September sky. Darkness followed very closely behind it. We decided not to waste the batteries in our torches, so we just sat there listening to the night sounds. There were still a few birds around, so there were still a few songs to be sung before they settled down for the night. Then there was just the wind in the trees and the odd rustle of some small animal in the heather. After that, there was mostly silence. Not total silence, but almost!

We all heard it at the same time - a distant droning noise. It was definitely not a sound from nature.

'I think it's the plane,' whispered Aretha.

'You don't need to whisper,' whispered Tara!

We all laughed, but all the same, nobody spoke. We just got up silently and picked up our backpacks.

'Go to the heather,' I whispered to the others and turned to Silke.

'Looks like we're on.'

'Go, Iago. Just try to make it easy for me! I vill delay him az long az I can.'

I turned and ran to the heather, as Silke got back inside her car.

I had just crouched below the soft purple bushes when I saw the plane's lights. Time stood still while the aircraft slowly approached the runway. The reflective lights on the small airstrip lit up as it drew nearer. We were all deadly still, holding our breaths, as the wheels touched down. The plane taxied towards the hangar. The engines powered down as the pilot got ready to go and collect Silke, who remained in her car. After a short while, the door of the aircraft opened and the pilot came out. He waved to Silke in her car, and walked towards her. Silke rolled down her window.

'Guten Abend, Hans,' I heard her say.

'Guten Abend Fräulein Schmidt,' came his reply.

I heard her begin to speak to him but I wasn't listening

anymore. Now it was time to act. I stood up, still keeping low and motioned to the others to follow. Leaving the safe cover of the heather, we ran silently towards the rear of the aircraft. Now, we were completely exposed. If Hans turned around it would all be over. Stopping just at the plane's tail, I raised my hand to halt the others, and felt Cam sliding in just behind me. Charlie was next, followed by Tara and Aretha, holding hands. Renny, as usual, brought up the rear; the string on his backpack was so long it was trailing along the ground as he ran. I shook my head, waiting for him to trip over it. By the smallest stroke of luck, he didn't and finally he joined the rest of us. We all stood there, catching our breath. It wasn't that it had been a very long run. Probably the adrenaline racing through our veins was making us breathe faster.

I braced myself; the most difficult part was still to come. Taking a long deep breath, I slipped carefully around the plane's tail. Crouched half way under the plane's belly, I crept forward almost silently. When I had reached the cover of the stairway, I motioned for the others to join me. They all copied my movements carefully this time, even Renny, whose bag had been seen to by Charlie. I peeped over the stairway to get a view of Silke and the pilot. Silke was still sitting in her car seat, facing me. Her door was open and I could just make out her face in the car's dim interior light. I couldn't tell if she could see my head, but as if on cue, she stepped out of the car and started walking towards the boot. The pilot followed. This was our chance. I whispered, 'NOW' and without a second glance, I ran to the foot of the steps. Standing at the bottom, I urged the others up the steps. Time ticked by and my pulse boomed loudly in my ears. It seemed to take forever. I dared not look behind me.

   Finally, when they were all inside the cabin, I turned to check on Silke. To my horror, the pilot was turning towards me, Silke's suitcase in his hands. I froze in terror. Was this it? Everyone else would go to Switzerland and I would be left behind, on an airstrip, in the middle of nowhere. Or worse still, I would be caught by the pilot and the rest soon discovered. Instinct made me crouch down low. Silke must have caught sight of me because as the pilot walked towards me, she almost screamed, 'Warte! Ich glaube ich habe Etwas vergessen.' I had no clue what she was shouting about, but the pilot turned back towards her. This was my one and only…my very last chance. I had to take it! 'No time for second thoughts now,' I thought. And closing my eyes in fear, I ran for it!

19
The Mattress

Diving commando-like inside the belly of the aircraft, I flopped hard onto the floor. Why did that always seem so easy in films? Maybe it was just that I was a wimp! There was no sign of the others. The cabin was in total darkness and they were all well hidden.

'Psst!' I heard from behind the second row of seats. Scrambling forward on my elbows and knees, I had just managed to drag my feet behind the chair, when I heard their voices on the stairs. The pilot jumped on board, with Silke close behind him. I couldn't understand what she was saying to him, but her voice sounded calm. I heard her drop down in the front seat and sigh, yawning, 'Ich bin müde, Hans. Kanst Du die Tür bitte schliessen?'

'Kein Problem,' replied Hans, closing the door.

My German isn't great, but I guessed she had asked him to close the door. Letting out a long sigh, I smiled at the gang. Charlie gave me the thumbs up and I surveyed the cabin. The plane was much smaller than I had thought so we would have to stay where we were for the flight.

'Psstt!' I whispered, sticking my head around the back of the chair. Silke turned her head and put her finger to her lips. She knew this plane well and had probably sat in the cockpit many times; the door wasn't totally soundproof. We all sat very still.

When the engines started and the pilot began his take-off manoeuvres, we relaxed. Silke got up from her seat and came to crouch between us. 'Ve forgot to talk about how ve vill get you off zis plane!' she started.

'Hadn't really thought that far, to be honest,' I replied.

'Vell, ve vill land near my house. I vill have to go directly to see my father. You vill need to stay very quiet vhile ze pilot locks ze plane. You vill be stuck here for a vhile, but I vill come to let you out as soon as I can. It might be tomorrow morning, but at least you vill have somewhere varm to sleep tonight. Zeese seats are very comfortable but zere are only five, zo one of you vill have to sleep on ze floor!' She smiled at Aretha and rubbed her head. She was taking good care of us, like she promised.

'Yey!' whispered Tara, 'a night on a plane!'

'Cool!' whispered Charlie.

'Better than camping outdoors, I suppose,' mumbled Cam.

I rolled my eyes - some people!

20
The Myriad

The plane touched down with a gentle bump. Silke jumped out of her seat while it taxied towards the small hangar. Sliding the cockpit door across she said something to the pilot, in German again, so I didn't catch it, but heard him reply 'OK.'

Bringing the plane to a stop. Silke watched from inside the plane as Hans jumped down and opened the hangar doors. Climbing back in, he taxied the plane inside the hangar. As soon as he'd switched off the engines and all the lights, he joined Silke. We heard a final slam as they headed out of the hangar. Their voices drifted off into the night.

All six of us let out a huge sigh of relief.

'One minute longer and I don't think my leg would have ever worked again,' said Charlie, as she tried to stand up. 'Owwww!' she squealed, her dead leg giving way beneath her. She stumbled backwards and I put my arms out to catch her. Her hair flopped over her face as she landed. Pushing it back absently, she looked into my face.

'Thanks Iago,' she mumbled, her cheeks colouring red. She was definitely a bit embarrassed.

'Oh no problem,' I replied, even more embarrassed. 'Oh

no problem,' I thought to myself. I sounded like an idiot. 'Well done Iago, that'll really impress her!'

'I don't know about you guys, but I'm starving!' said Renny from the back of the plane. It was 10.25pm local time by my watch, and in all the excitement, none of us had remembered to eat before we left, not counting Aretha's salt binge.

'Check out the kitchen arrangements,' I said to Renny.

'I think you mean the galley,' sniggered Tara, teasing me.

'OK, Miss Air Hostess! Since you seem to know so much about it, you can go and check out the galley!' I replied, sarcastically.

'Hmmphh!' moaned Tara dragging herself to her feet. 'I suppose that's what I get for being a smart-mouth!' She trundled off to join Renny at the back of the plane. Aretha got up. 'I think I'll go have a mooch round, see what I can find,' she smiled.

Cam, Charlie, and I looked at each other. 'I suppose this means we'd better get on and do something?' I said, unenthused. They both nodded their heads.

'Cam did you and Renny get the blueprints we needed?'

'Yeah, some of them,' he replied, 'but we can log on to the CERN website for anything we're missing. They have pretty good schematics of the LHC on it.' He pulled out his phone. 'How very helpful of them!' I smiled. He quickly logged on to the CERN page and we began to search through their schematics.

'What we need to work out is where, in this 27 kilometre long tunnel, your dad's fail-safe is located. Once we figure that out, we need to find a way to get to it. Any ideas?' I looked at Cam, hopefully.

'RENNY,' shouted Cam, suddenly. Charlie and I jumped slightly - we weren't expecting it.

'Shhhh!' I whispered crossly to Cam.

'Sorry!' he winced.

Renny stepped backwards out of the small galley area. He was wearing an apron! We all smirked.

'What's so funny?' he asked, looking down at his apron. 'It was there and I'm preparing food. What's so weird about that?' He was probably right. It was quite sensible, but that didn't stop him looking like a nerd.

'If the Cabin Crew can spare you, we need you here!' Cam's reply was dripping with sarcasm.

'Oh, yeah, right!' said Renny, removing his apron. Sometimes you had to love him; he didn't even notice when people made fun of him. He was just so enthusiastic about everything, and so good-natured. Grabbing his backpack, he flopped down beside Charlie and began carefully unrolling the blueprints he had found in his dad's office. The first few he pulled out were close up drawings of the magnet array and component parts. We didn't need that detail just yet, if ever.

'No... No... No...,' repeated Renny, as he went through the drawings. The pile of "no's" was starting to build up. There were only a few drawings left. My heart started to race again. I looked at Charlie. Her brow was furrowed; she was nervous too. I almost wanted to reach out and grab the last few drawings from Renny and rifle through them myself. Instead, I shifted and sat on my hands to control them. Cam groaned in frustration. Renny looked up. 'Hey don't start on me!' he moaned. 'None of you even know what to look for!' He was right. He was the only one who could do this bit and we should have been glad we had him. He put his head down and carried on. The three of us sat there in silence. We all held our breath.

'GOTCHA!' he squealed, as he held the second to last blueprint in the air. The tension broke and we all breathed out loudly. He spread the crumpled piece of paper on the floor between us. 'This is where Dad said his fail-safe is located.' Renny pointed to a section on a map. 'It's somewhere near the ALiCE detector. The only problem is that I don't know where exactly!' He looked up at us sheepishly. I stared hard at him.

'How many kilometres are you estimating when you say "don't know where, exactly?"'

'Could be 5... maybe 10...,' his voice trailed off.

'You mean we have to search up to 10km of an underground tunnel, looking for a colour code sequence!' I shouted.

'Calm down, Iago,' shushed Charlie, 'no-one said this would be easy!' She smiled at Renny saying, 'go on...' Renny blushed. Charlie even had that effect on him!

'Well, the good news is that once we have located the fail-safe, I do have the code we need to operate it.'

'So... what's the bad news then,' mumbled Cam.

'Apart from how do we get into CERN and how do we find the fail-safe, you mean!' I replied jokingly.

'Yeah, we do need to work on those things. But even if we manage to do all that, we might still have one major problem... Dad's shutdown operation needs major processing power. You see he was relying on The Grid to help him.'

'What's The Grid?' asked Charlie, getting in before Cam or I could.

Renny smiled again. I suppose that sometimes being a

boffin can have its rewards.

'Well,' he winked, cupping his hands behind his head and laying back... 'The Grid is a giant computer network. Basically, the people at CERN need much more processing power than they have, to run their experiments. So they set up a grid. You can connect your home computer to "The GRID" via the internet. Then, the spare processing power in your computer can then be used by CERN, for their experiments.'

'Wow!' said Charlie, 'so experiments into the birth of the universe could be running on your computer at home!'

'Well, in a round about way - yes!' replied Renny smugly. 'You see Dad didn't think for one minute that he mightn't have access to The GRID. Who would have guessed he'd end up "banged up"?'

We all laughed. Nobody was less likely to be suspected of a criminal offence than Uncle Jonas. Then Cam and I looked at each other seriously. For a while, we'd forgotten about both our fathers and why we were doing this.

'Renny,' I said, confidently, 'let's not worry about The Grid at this point in time. We will find a way. Let's just focus on getting into CERN and finding your Dad's off-switch, for now!'

'The entrance to CERN is at Meyrin, near the airport,' said Cam, looking up from the screen of his phone. I pulled out the map pages I had brought. I felt a bit of a dinosaur but sometimes it is easier to look on a big piece of paper than a small screen. 'OK, we're about 7km from there. Might have a bit of a hike tomorrow, so we'd better eat something and get some sleep,' I said yawning.

'Oi where's the food?' Charlie shouted in the direction of the galley.

21
The Mmmmmm...

'Coming!' came the voice of a flustered Tara from the cabin.

Aretha came rushing through with a picnic blanket she had found. She spread it on the floor, just behind the chairs. Following close behind her, with a tray of steaming mugs, came Tara. She put the tray down with a, 'Ta-daa!'

'Tomato soup?' exclaimed Renny.

'Who goes on an adventure without tomato soup?' smiled Tara.

'Tar', you're just fabulous,' said Charlie, cuddling the younger girl, 'I don't suppose you remembered to bring the cocoa as well!'

'I did,' said Tara frowning, 'but we haven't got any milk! Sorry!'

'Oh, never mind,' said Charlie, 'I've brought crackers!'

We all searched through our backpacks to see what we could come up with to accompany the soup. Soon the middle of the picnic blanket was piled high with cheese strings, cocktail sausages, sliced ham, bread rolls, sausage rolls, and tins of tuna.

'Oh wait,' smiled Tara running back to the galley. 'OK - dive in,' she said, as she returned with plates and knives.

We all began to tuck in like vultures that haven't eaten in a while. By the time we had finished, there were only crumbs left on the blanket.

'Come on Cam,' I said, getting up, 'I guess it's our turn to do the washing up.'

Cam mumbled something but he got up anyway. I suppose that, with a mum like Auntie Meg, you don't have to help much around the kitchen. Charlie went to help the girls settle down and Renny slumped in a chair, with Uncle Jonas's files.

Cam carried some dishes and cups to me and I started to wash up in the tiny sink.

Bringing the last of them, he stood by the doorframe with his back to the others.

'I'm a bit worried about the younger ones,' he said, very quietly. 'I'm not sure we should take them any further.' I carried on with the washing up wordlessly, while I thought about this. He was probably right, but I wouldn't want to be the one to tell them. 'I know what you're thinking,' he grimaced, 'Tara would probably flip!'

'Maybe we can find something less dangerous, but still important for them,' I said, after a while. 'Let's sleep on it!'

'Heads or tails,' said Cam, coolly tossing a coin in the air.

'For what?' I replied, puzzled.

'Just call it, Iago.'

'Tails,' I replied quickly.

'Hard luck,' he smirked, walking back into the cabin. I watched him flop down, reclining his chair to almost flat.

'Pah!' I threw down the tea towel angrily.

Grabbing the picnic blanket, I shook it roughly and

spread it on the floor. It wouldn't make the floor any softer but it was, at least, something to lie on. Dragging my bag under my head, I tried to get comfortable.

Charlie kissed Tara and Aretha, who were sleeping in the front seats, before settling down in the chair just in front of me. She reclined her chair back and rolled over to talk to me. Lying on her tummy, she smiled. 'The girls are having such fun,' she said, 'but I am a bit worried about them.'

'Cam and I just had this discussion,' I whispered back. 'I'll do my best to keep them safe.'

'I know you will, Iago,' she said, reaching her hand out and ruffling my hair. 'Goodnight!' she yawned, rolling onto her side. Now I could only see the top of her head, her long dark hair flowing over the end of the seat.

I lay there awake for hours, just going over all the events in my head. I was way too wound-up for sleep. Then Charlie turned over in her seat, letting her hand fall limply, right in front of me. On instinct, I reached up and touched it. It was so soft. I just lay there for a while feeling her soft warm hand in mine. My eyes closed and I must have drifted off.

I awoke with a start. Opening my eyes, a blurry image seemed to be swaying in front of me. It was Tara. She was bending down in front of me, smiling. I sat up and almost died of embarrassment when I realised I was still holding Charlie's hand.

'Aww, how cute!' grinned Tara.

'What are you doing Tara?' I asked, groggily.

'I was going to the bathroom. More to the point, what were you doing?' she teased.

'Tara, if you breathe a word!' I hissed through gritted

teeth.

'I won't, lover boy!' she whispered and headed back to her seat.

22

The Unexpected Peace

It was still dark when Silke tapped softly on the door. Although we knew it had to be her, we all sat up and held our breath. Aretha squealed and ran to her, as soon as she saw her blonde head entering the cabin. Again, I worried about Aretha and wanted to keep her out of harm's way. That might be a bit harder after what Tara had seen last night. Tara was smart; she would use it to manipulate me! I would have to outsmart Miss Smartypants!

'Silke, have you got a car you can use?' I asked as soon as she had shut the door.

'Of course, Iago,' she replied, smiling.

'Phew, that saves us a 7 km walk today!' I looked around, grinning. 'OK, where can you pick us up? It needs to be somewhere where we won't be spotted.'

Silke bent her head, thinking. 'I zink it's best if you make your way over ze small hill, behind ze hangar and through ze little wood. Ze road passes ze side of ze wood. I could stop to pick you up vizout being seen.'

'We'd better leave soon,' I said looking around at the others, 'before it gets too light.'

'Silke when will you be able to meet us?' Cam asked hopefully.

'I vill have to eat breakfast vith my father, but he wakes early and leaves early, so I should be finished in less zan two hours.' She looked at her watch. 'I should be able to meet you at eight o'clock. Is zat OK?'

'Great! Now, go before they see you!' I said, physically turning her towards the door.

'See you later,' she whispered and ran softly back towards the house.

'We've got a bit of time to kill,' I said, 'so while we each take our turn in the bathroom, the others should do some investigating. We need to find a way of getting into CERN.

Charlie went to the small bathroom first. We all watched her go and only after she had shut the door we got to work. I got out my phone and opened my browser. I typed in "CERN security" and in 0.28 seconds, I got back 2700 results. Scanning down the page, one of the titles caught my eye. Following the link "Hackers breach CERN security," I began to speed read. The story was about the Greek Security Team - some hackers from Greece who had managed to break into an important webpage at CERN. Apparently, they were only one step away from the program which controls the LHC. I looked up from my screen, astonished.

'Renny, Cam, you seen this?' I asked quietly. Cam ignored me; he seemed to be totally wrapped up in something on his screen. Renny shuffled over and peeped at my screen. 'Yeah, cool huh?' he snickered. 'Read about it! You should have read the blogs; they were heroes, just for one day.'

'Renny?' I asked, turning my head towards him, as the screws in my mind turned. 'Do you think it would be possible to leave a message for the Greek Security Team on a blog somewhere?' Renny scratched his head, 'I would have to post on a few, but if they've got a "sweeper" out there, they should pick it up. What do you want to ask them?'

'For their help!' I grinned. 'If they can get into CERN's systems, then surely they can help us access the main security grid. Who knows what else they can do for us?'

'Yeah,' grinned Renny as the penny dropped. 'Yeah dude...I'll get on it.' He flopped down opposite me.

'Don't get so carried away you forget to wash yourself!' I joked. Renny needed to be reminded about personal hygiene!

Charlie emerged from the small bathroom and Tara and Aretha raced each other to get there. Of course, Tara got there first, but a quick glare from Charlie made her offer to let Aretha have first turn. Tara skulked back to her seat. She picked up her phone and started typing.

'Hey Iago,' she called, 'looks like they're having an open day at the computer centre today.'

'At CERN?' I asked, surprised.

'No, at the Kennedy Space Centre...! Of course at CERN, idiot!' The last word was almost whispered under her breath. I sat up suddenly; this was just too good to be true. Swivelling her screen towards me, she grinned triumphantly. Miss Smartypants had just solved one of my problems.

Grinning smugly in her direction, I said, 'Tara, this one is made for you and Aretha. Silke can take you to the open day. Who would ever suspect two sweet girls and their au pair? Of course it will be deep cover,' I laughed, 'you'll actually have to pretend to be a sweet girl!' My cousin punched me hard in the arm. 'See what I mean!' I joked, though I made sure I stepped away from her this time. She could be really mean, sometimes.

A crash somewhere just behind me made me jump. Turning my head, I saw Cam banging his fist against the side of the plane and Charlie trying to comfort him.

'What is it Cam?' I asked, unsure whether I wanted to hear the answer.

23

The Unhinged

'You'd better check it out yourself,' said Charlie, picking up Cam's Phone and handing it to me. Cam's inbox was open and a message had come through via his Facebook wall. There was an MP4 file attached to the mail – no title – just three dots. Nervously I clicked the file open.

I shrank back in horror as the hideous face filled the screen. Her large yellow crooked teeth took up at least one third of her face and the huge glasses she wore pretty much covered the rest. If the teeth were anything to go by, that was probably a good thing! She sort of, snorted and then cackled into the camera. Then she stepped back slightly. I could now see the rest of her head and shoulders. Her hair was dyed bright red and some of it hung in clumps around her ugly face, while other bits stuck straight up in the air. All in all, I'd have to say, she was the ugliest creature I had ever seen. Then she started talking…

'Where a long haired English rock band with a rainbow colour name, came to make deep music we start our little game. Where once Lord Byron's "prisoner" had a nice view of a lake, you'll find the way to guide you to the next step you must take.'

She paused and I waited, knowing in my heart of hearts that this could only be one person: Katarina Kreng.

'Hurry now, Cameron. Your Uncle's counting on you!' said the hag, as she moved closer to the camera. Then she was gone.

I sunk to my knees and let my head fall into my hands. 'Oh God, she knows!'

Charlie came to me, and sinking slowly down beside me, stroked my hair gently. Even that didn't make me feel any better. I was terrified. That witch obviously knew that she had the wrong brother. Since she didn't need him, it seemed she had decided to play a game with him. If she was as twisted as Uncle Jonas said she was, who knew what she might do to him? The last happy image of Dad I had, flashed through my mind; Aretha hugging him by the car. Oh my god - Aretha! She mustn't know about this. I stood up quickly. I didn't have much time. Thank God, she had been in the bathroom when Cam got the message.

'Tara,' I whispered, 'you've got to keep this from her!'

'Of course I will, Iago,' Tara whispered back.

'You need to distract her, while we think.'

'Well, I can't exactly take her shopping. Can I?' whispered Tara, sarcastically.

'Charlie...?' I asked hopefully.

'When Tara's had her wash, we girls will put together some breakfast. How's that?' smiled Charlie, leading a still glowering Tara towards the bathroom.

'Renny keep doing what you're doing!' I said quickly.

'Mmmmm,' muttered Renny, barely lifting his head. He was deep in nerd-world now and hardly noticed what was going on.

'Iago,' whispered Cam, 'do you think that witch knows

where we are. I mean why did she send that message?' He looked around the cabin, thinking. 'And also, why did she send it to me, not you?'

I thought about his questions for a while. They were good questions. Slowly the cogs in my brain started turning. I couldn't answer the first question. I didn't know if she knew where we were but if her henchmen had been watching us then that was very possible. But, I did know the answer to the second question. 'She doesn't know who Aretha and I are,' I began. Cam frowned at me, confused. 'Well, she did her homework on your Dad and his family, but not mine.'

'Of course,' replied Cam, 'and she must have found my number in Uncle Greg's phone! She knows I'm here. I have to be the one who goes looking for him then. With any luck, her henchmen will follow me. Maybe you guys won't be followed.'

'Maybe,' I replied, shrugging my shoulders, but I wasn't very hopeful. 'We'd better start trying to solve her riddle then. What did she mean?'

Cam was already googling 'English rock band&deep&music&lake'. He scrolled through the results… Nothing! 'OK,' he said, 'the answer's not going to jump out at us, no matter how long we search. I'll have to do some thinking… On my own!' I was a bit miffed to be dismissed so easily. But he was right. Sometimes it was easier to think without someone else peering over your shoulder. Besides, I had other things to think about, anyway!

'Iago,' called Renny, waving me over with his left hand, his right hand continuing to type furiously.

'You got something already?' I asked, crouching down

beside him.

'Well, I've got a friend who works for Microsoft as a hacker…'

'What…they employ hackers at Microsoft now?' I interrupted, raising my eyebrows so high, my forehead hurt. 'And you've got a friend…?' I laughed.

'Not funny, Iago,' replied Renny, looking hurt.

'Sorry Man!' I said, raising my hand in a peace gesture.

'Anyway, my friend - who I met through RuneScape years ago,' he continued, 'is what's called a "white hat hacker". He tests Microsoft code before it goes out into the great unknown. He used to be on the "outside" but he got into a bit of trouble and… well, let's just say he was persuaded to "see the light" at Microsoft!' Again, Renny grinned smugly, as if by knowing someone that cool made him cool too! I had no choice but to hit him lightly on the top of the head, to bring him back to reality.

'What's that for?' he whined.

'Get on with it Renny!' I said, a bit gruffly.

'Anyway "spottytechfreak" got back to me. He knows how to communicate directly with the Greek Security Team. He won't give me the details but he will pass on my message… Paranoid technobaby! So, I've just sent the file. Now, all we can do is, wait for their response.'

'Good work Renny. I just hope they don't take too long,' I said, rubbing my head.

'Yeah, probably too paranoid to even reply,' replied Renny, sagging back in his chair. 'They probably think Interpol, or the CIA, are after them!'

'We can only hope…' I replied, drifting over towards Cam.

'Any luck?' I asked.

'Nah!' he huffed. I looked around. The girls had finished in the bathroom, so I decided to take my turn.

As I squeezed past the galley, the delicious smell of brewing coffee hit me. I looked across at Charlie, who looked up at me, smiling. My mind went blank and I sort of stumbled into the small bathroom. God, why did I do that every time she smiled at me! I felt like such an idiot. I banged my head against the mirror in frustration. Control yourself Iago!

24
The Unchained Melody

When I left the tiny bathroom, the others were already sitting down to coffee and biscuits. Not exactly the healthiest breakfast, but it would have to do. Charlie handed me a cup and I drank it down gratefully. Cam shoved another whole biscuit into his mouth, and shuffled off to take his turn in the bathroom. Looking directly at Charlie, I signalled that I needed to speak to her - alone. She sidled across the plane, trying to make it look like she just wanted a casual chat. Tara picked up on it, immediately turning to Aretha. 'Come on, let's clear up girl,' she moaned. She stood up and picked up some cups, 'At least then, we won't have to do the washing up!' She glared at Charlie and me.

'Don't worry Tara,' I said smiling sweetly at her. 'We'll do it'

Charlie's eyebrows shot up. Me, volunteering to do something for myself, surprised her. I was a bit hurt; I wasn't that lazy! Was I? I took the cups from the girls and deliberately made my way to the sink. I have to admit that I did a bit of crashing and banging and that maybe I overdid it a bit. Then I remembered my Dad and stopped acting like an idiot.

'Did Cam figure anything out yet?' I asked her, quietly.

'Not that he told me, anyway,' she replied, drying the cup I handed to her.

'Dun dun dun, dun dun, de-dun. Dun dun dun, dun dun,' came the sound of Cam's humming from the washroom. We both looked at each other, surprised. Then we heard a muffled shout of, 'That's it!' and a second later the door burst open. There stood Cam, with only a towel wrapped around his waist. Charlie stepped back, a bit shocked.

Cam looked down. 'Oh sorry,' he smiled, stepping back behind the small door. Now just his head was sticking around it. 'It's just that I've figured it out!'

'Figured what out,' said Aretha coming to see what was going on.

'Oh, just a puzzle,' I said, glancing at Cam. 'Nothing important! Go pack your bag Aretha, we need to leave soon.'

'OK Iago,' she mumbled sadly. 'I know when I'm not wanted.' She shuffled off with her head hanging low. I felt awful, but I couldn't let her know.

'What is it?' I whispered to Cam, once she was out of earshot.

'It's Deep Purple!' he replied, excitedly.

Charlie frowned. 'What's deep purple?' she said, looking around.

'The English rock band!' whispered Cam, grinning.

'Why Deep Purple?' asked Charlie.

'Smoke on the Water,' he replied.

'Again, what's that?' asked Charlie, her hand on her hip.

'It's a song by Deep Purple and the first line goes… "We all went down to Montreaux, on the lake Geneva shore", or something like that…' he replied.

'And?' I didn't get the connection.

'Well, Lake Geneva isn't far from here. That's what the first line of that hag's message is about! Now we just need to find out what the second line means.'

'Brilliant Cam!' I said. 'Now hurry up and get dressed. Let's see what else we can find.' Cam hurried back inside the small bathroom and came out in less than a minute, his jeans on, but carrying his t-shirt and socks in his hand. Flopping down in his seat, he grabbed his phone and started searching straight away. When Cam was on to something, there was no stopping him.

25
The Underpinning

While Cam went on trying to work out the second line of the puzzle, I gathered the others round. 'Silke will be here soon, so we need to be ready to leave. Is everyone packed?' They all nodded their heads. 'Good. OK. So, here's the plan: Tara and Aretha - you go with Silke to the open day at the Computer Centre. Renny will need you to be ready as soon as we access Uncle Jonas's safety switch. I can't tell you exactly what you need to do when you get there but I think you need to just, hang around. Renny - you go with the girls but you need to stay outside the computer centre. Keep working on your hacker friends; hopefully they can get us inside CERN.' I stopped for just a second.

'Charlie and I will go to the Globe exhibition centre. It's right near Entrance A. We can sign up for a tour of the Main Building. As soon as you let us know where we can enter, we will be ready to go.'

'And Cam?' asked Aretha, pointing in his direction.

'Uhmmm, well Cam's working on something else, at the moment. I don't really want to interfere, you know what I mean!' I gave her a look of fear. Aretha bought it; she knew that relations were often strained between Cam and me. I gave them all a broad smile. I didn't really feel like their brave and fearless leader, but I couldn't let them know that. They needed me to be strong.

Renny went back to his blogs and Charlie and I walked back towards Cam. Very quietly, I asked 'Did you figure out the second line yet?'

He turned his small screen towards me. He had googled "Lord Byron&prisoner&lake Geneva" and the results all showed one place: The Chateau de Chillon. He followed the official link www.chillon.ch. It was an ancient castle, right on the edge of Lake Geneva. It looked beautiful but old, and cold and damp. I thought of my dad being held prisoner there and a shiver went down my spine. My face must have shown it because Charlie touched my arm gently. Cam looked up when he saw her do this and his eyes flashed angrily for a split second. Then he saw the fear in my eyes and his look changed. He leaned forward and put his hand on my shoulder whispering, 'Don't worry Man, I will find him!'

That was settled then. Cam would not come with us. Instead, he would follow the clues left by the Kreng hag and he would find my father. I felt bad that I wasn't the one going to look for my dad, but Cam was much better at that kind of thing than I was. I got bored by level 3 of most games, but Cam could keep going for days on end. And besides - there was another, equally important job to be done. We didn't know when or how Katarina Kreng was going to strike but we had only one chance to stop her.

We needed to get a move on; there's no point closing the stable door after the horse has bolted. Renny needed to come up with the goods. I was starting to feel stressed and a bit cooped up. It's great to be able to do lots of research on your computer or mobile phone but sometimes you need to get out there; get some air in your lungs, see the sky, feel the rain. I needed to leave… And soon!

26
The Up n' at 'em

'OK troops, let's go!' I said, checking my watch. It was still only 7.30, but we were due to meet Silke by the road at around 8 o'clock.

Renny moaned, 'But I'm still working!'

'And you haven't had a wash!' said Charlie.

'Renny, get in that bathroom now!' I shouted. 'You've got ten seconds...' Renny scrambled to the back of the plane. Lord knows how much cleaning he would do in ten seconds... not much - but better than nothing!

The rest of us picked up our bags and put them by the door. Then, while Cam and the girls waited, Charlie and I went around the cabin, just making sure that everything was exactly where it should be. Someone might eventually notice that the coffee level had dropped quite a bit, but hopefully, not for a few days.

Renny flung the door of the bathroom open and raced towards the pile of bags, wearing nothing but a towel. 'Underpants,' he said bashfully, rifling through his bag. We all laughed! At least this time he had remembered to bring some.

'Dress here!' said Charlie. 'I'll go and tidy up the washroom.'

Renny looked at everyone sheepishly. 'Well, there's no need for everyone to stare!' he snapped. We all turned our backs, still sniggering.

Five minutes later, I closed the aircraft door and joined the others by the small side door of the hangar. I nodded at Cam. Gingerly opening the door, he stuck his head out, just a little bit. He quickly scanned left to right and ducked back inside the door. I looked at him anxiously. 'There are a few people about,' he whispered. 'I can see the limo at the front of the house and it sounds like the engine's running.'

'That'll be waiting to take Silke's dad to his office.' I quickly replied.

'I can see some other people moving about, but they're not too close. I'd say they are probably gardeners. I think…'

Cam's next word was drowned out by a loud metallic sound. We all wheeled around in shock…Someone was opening the big hangar doors. Could it be Silke? But why would Silke be opening those doors? No, the only person who would need to open those doors would be someone who wanted to get a plane out… The pilot!

Without a word, I pushed Cam forward. Catching hold of Tara and Aretha, who were now closest to the door, he pulled them through. Charlie grabbed Renny and I dived through the doorway behind them. I landed really heavily on the dirt just as Cam quietly closed the door behind me. Though my knees hurt and my ribs ached, I kept my mouth firmly closed. We all stood dead still. Hopefully we had been lucky. I prayed that the pilot hadn't noticed us. I dragged myself silently to my feet.

Then we heard a faint, 'Hallo?' from inside the hangar.

Drat, we hadn't been lucky then. No time for planning now. Looking around, I saw the small woods that Silke had mentioned and I ran. Glancing over my shoulder, I saw Charlie grab the girls and soon they were flying. Within five seconds, she had passed me - the girls' shorter legs moving twice as fast to keep up with hers. As I said, she could run!

We reached the edge of the small copse a few seconds later. Just as Renny, the last of us, dived behind a rather skinny tree, the small side door to the hangar flew open. The sound of the door crashing against the aluminium sides of the hangar made me jump. We all looked on nervously as the pilot scanned the surrounding area. He stood there for a few more minutes, looking around and listening. Then we heard him mutter something and go back inside the hangar. We all breathed a sigh of relief.

I checked my watch - quarter to eight. 'Let's go!' I whispered and Aretha came up and grabbed my hand. 'Phew, that was a bit exciting,' she said, her eyes gleaming.

'Little adrenaline junky!' I said, pushing her forward playfully.

We moved off quietly, keeping our eyes peeled for any movement in the woods. It would be stupid to get caught now by a tree surgeon or something. Cam was on point and I hung back, to make sure that there were no surprises from behind. The woods were quite crunchy underfoot and very overgrown. We had to push our way through dense bushes and climb over fallen branches, but eventually we could see light. This meant we were nearing a clearing. I hoped it was the road. My hands were scratched and my knees were bleeding from my earlier dive. I really didn't feel like wandering around in a wood all morning.

'This way,' came Cam's voice, barely above a whisper. He was heading to his left. We followed, and gradually the sound of a car engine ticking over became louder. By the time I reached the road, Cam already had the car door open and Tara and Aretha were climbing inside the Land Rover.

'Iago, I'm soooo sorry,' came Silke's voice. 'I had no idea that the pilot was going anywhere today. Vhen my dad told me, it was too late to varn you!'

'I'll forgive you Silke but only if you've got some plasters!' I smiled at her.

'Zere is a medical kit in ze back,' she said.

Cam jumped in the front seat beside Silke. 'You need to drop me at the station,' he said quietly. Silke's looked at him puzzled. Cam shook his head ever so slightly. She understood. She knew not to ask any further. She turned her attention back to Charlie and me. 'You two vill have to ride in ze back for a while. Get in Renny!' she shouted and Renny, who had been typing furiously, jumped in without even looking up. 'Strap him in Tara!' said Silke. She knew Renny wouldn't bother and she was committed to keeping us safe.

27
The Unravelling

Charlie and I scrambled into the back of the Land Rover, as Silke put her foot down. We hadn't had time to strap ourselves into the tiny side seats yet, so we both lurched forward, or rather backwards, bumping painfully against the rear door. 'Owww! Silke!' I shouted. I was in enough pain already.

'Oops, sorry,' Silke said, waving to us in the rear-view mirror. Then she slowed down a bit.

Charlie and I strapped ourselves in and I reached for the medical box. 'Here, let me have a look,' said Charlie seriously. I rolled my trousers up above my knee. She flinched and I looked down at my knee, feeling sorry for myself. It was a bit of a mess. My jeans had ripped when I had dived, and after trudging through the woods there were all kinds of things stuck inside the cut. Charlie got out something that looked like dettol and some gauze. She put the liquid on the gauze and gently tried to clean my wound. 'Aaaaooowwww!' I screeched, as the disinfectant came in contact with raw flesh. Then I looked over at Charlie. She did not look impressed, so I decided to suck it up! After a few excruciating minutes, the wound was cleaned to her satisfaction, so she smeared some cream over it and cut a big strip of plaster. Looking up at me she smiled, 'Brave Iago!' Then she smoothed the sticky bits of the plaster over my knee. I looked at her quizzically. Was she making fun of me? I never could tell with Charlie.

As soon as we arrived at the train station, Cam jumped out.

'Vat about money?' asked Silke as he grabbed his bag. 'Got a bankcard, haven't I!' replied Cam as he slammed the door.

He came around to the back and opened the door.

'Iago, I'll try to keep in touch. Let me know if you hear from…' he tilted his head sideways. I knew what he meant. If the Kreng witch decided to contact one of us, Cam needed to know about it.

'Likewise,' I said, 'and when you get to the next level let me know!'

'Seeya then,' he said, giving Charlie a small smile. Suddenly he seemed young and alone. No, mustn't think like that! Otherwise, we might as well give up right here! I shook my head and watched Cam run up the station steps. He didn't speak any German but his French was OK. I was sure I could count on him to get to Montreaux.

As soon as Cam disappeared inside the station, Silke drove off. She turned on her GPS and entered CERN as the destination. Then she put on some music and we all relaxed a little; there was not much else we could do. After a while, I noticed Renny's hand appearing over the back of his seat. He was holding his phone and waving it about. I took it from him and Charlie dropped her head to one side in question. The screen was totally black with a green font that read…'frm GRK hkrs…cn axss dr – grd rf 218b. B thr 11h. 5mn wndw.' I handed it to Charlie silently.

She shrugged her shoulders saying, 'all geek to me!' So neither of us knew what it meant. Only Renny could decipher shorthand geek!

Leaning over the seat back, I tapped him quite hard on the head. He whined, but I think he knew it was coming. He swivelled around.

'What?' he said raising his hands, in question.

I gritted my teeth and spat, 'Translate!' He smiled.

'Can you believe it, that's actually a message from the guys who hacked CERN? I'm never gonna delete it,' and then he grabbed his phone from me.

'Aaaawwww!' he whined, staring at the screen in disbelief. He turned it towards me. The message was gone.

'Come on Renny. Guys who are clever enough to hack their way into CERN are not going to leave a message that you can save and show your pals, are they?'

'S'pose not!' he said sadly, slumping back in his seat.

'So, what did the message mean?'

'Oh yeah,' he said unenthusiastically, 'they'll have door 218b open for you at 11'o clock. You've got five minutes to get in, before it locks itself again.'

I sighed, so this was really going to happen then. So far, it had seemed unlikely. But now, we had a way in. I was feeling a bit better now, though still unbelievably nervous. But I wouldn't let it show - certainly not in front of Charlie. So I sat back, smiled, and tried to look like I was relaxing for the rest of the journey…

Silke arrived at the GPS coordinates she had input and screeched to a halt, as usual. I was beginning to wonder if she'd even taken a driving test. The instructor had probably passed her out of sheer terror, no doubt desperate to get out of the car. I know I was!

Charlie and I were first to escape, followed quickly by the others. Silke's driving was frightening in the quiet English countryside, but in a huge European city, she was truly terrifying. 'Phew,' said Tara, mock wiping her brow, 'don't know what we face today but nothing could be more terrifying than that!' Somehow, I didn't think Tara was right, but I didn't want to frighten her. 'Yeah Tar' – just a walk in the park!' I said, smiling.

Silke went to pay the parking, so I gathered the "gang" around. 'OK everyone; this will be our last group meeting. After this, we go our separate ways. Does everybody have what he or she needs? ...Aretha?'

Aretha grinned, but she humoured me. 'Money – check, friends – check, phone – check, chocolate – check. Hey, that sounds like that John Mayer song Dad plays!' She started singing, 'Why is it everything I think I need always comes with batteries?' She was actually a pretty good singer – I reminded myself to tell her that one day but the last word she sang hung in the air. None of us had thought of recharging our batteries. I checked mine; half-full. 'We'll have to be careful with our batteries,' I said holding my phone up. Aretha looked at hers. 'Yikes!' she said, frowning.

'Don't you guys ever watch The Gadget Show,' smirked Renny, detaching a small silver device from his belt. It was about two inches long and we watched as he inserted a connector into the device.

'What is it?' asked Charlie.

'It's an emergency phone charger,' Renny replied, plugging it into his phone's charger socket. It runs on normal AAA batteries and can last for up to four hours.'

'Wow,' said Tara. 'What a great idea!'

'The only problem,' Renny continued, 'is I only have one.'

'Iago should have it,' was Charlie's instant reply.

I looked directly into her eyes. I was suddenly worried about her being somewhere alone, unable to contact anyone. But then – she would be with me, so why was I worried. I wouldn't let anything happen to her.

'OK,' I said, taking the charger from Renny, and clipping it to my belt. 'Tara, Aretha, charge your phones wherever you can!'

Silke came back with the parking ticket. 'Zis car park closes at 8pm,' she said, anxiously. She looked at me for advice.

I frowned. 'I hope that we manage to arm the fail-safe long before then!' I replied, cheerfully. I hoped my fake optimism had the desired effect.

'Renny, you go in with the girls. Check out the system and anything else you think might be important and then leave – remember, we'll need you on the outside. Girls, try to snoop around a bit. Look for places where you can hang out without looking suspicious. Just make sure you're there when Renny needs you.' I hugged my sister, and then messed up Tara's hair before turning to Renny. 'Please get the communications part of this sorted out. There's no point in Charlie and me getting in there if you can't give us the processing power we need! We need The GRID.'

'But last night you said not to worry about that…you said we'd deal with that later!' he whined.

'This *is* later Renny!'

28
The Unpleasant

Renny looked scared for the first time but I couldn't stand around holding his hand. Charlie and I needed to get to door 218b before 11am and we didn't even have a clue where that was. I waved back at the others as we went towards The Globe - the exhibition centre at CERN. Charlie had Uncle Jonas's schematics rolled up in her small backpack. We stopped to check them before we entered the building. It probably wasn't too smart to be seen walking around the building, following a schematic blueprint. I didn't know what level of security they had at CERN, but I was pretty sure that even the worst security guard might notice that! It took a few minutes but I found the location of the door. I tried to memorise as much as I could of the interior layout of the main building.

Arriving at The Globe's reception desk, we signed up for the 9.30am tour of the Main Building. We would have to find a way to slip away from the Group. I hoped we would have enough time. There was nothing I could do now but be patient.

Charlie was pacing up and down the reception area nervously. Patience wasn't her strong point! At first, I didn't pay much attention to her. That was just Charlie. She never sat or stood still. It was only after a few moments of watching her that I started to look around. I was worried that someone else might notice her. She was being a bit conspicuous. I was just about to approach her when I noticed a man. At least, I thought it was a man - right in the far corner of the large reception room. He wasn't watching Charlie, which was a bit odd, since almost every other man between the age of ten and seventy was. Charlie was, kind of, hard to miss! This man was slightly stooped and he seemed to be arguing quietly with himself. He was definitely a weirdo.

The Group Tour leader arrived in the Reception area and gave us all our access badges. Charlie started pinning mine to my shirt, and I didn't try to stop her. The light sensation of her fingers on my chest, made me close my eyes. I didn't want to open them again. I just wanted to stay here in this moment, a while longer.

A strange snuffling sound behind my shoulder dragged me back to reality. I looked down at Charlie. It must have shown on my face because, Charlie silently mouthed, 'What?'

I didn't have to look; I knew who was standing behind me: the weird man! Oh no, he was going to be in our group! How awful. Now that he was this close to me, I thought he even smelled a bit strange. Charlie wrinkled her nose and sniffed lightly. She screwed her face up in disgust! So she could smell it too.

I wanted to get away from this creature but I didn't want to be too obvious. Smiling down at Charlie, I put my arm around her shoulder. I hugged her close, like boyfriend and girlfriend and guided her towards the back of the group. Charlie caught on and giggled, snuggling her head against my body. She was too good at this acting. I, on the other hand, wasn't acting, at all! For several reasons, I decided that it would be best to keep up our boyfriend/girlfriend act!

Following the Group Leader, we headed towards the Main Building. She gave us the usual history info: when the CERN was formed, the original purpose of CERN, how the "World Wide Web" was invented here in 1992 by Sir Tim Berners-Lee and Robert Calliau. And finally, the LHC details, and some of what the scientists hoped to discover during their experiments.

Although Charlie and I knew some of the information, we had no idea that the internet had been invented here. We had been so focussed on our mission, that we hadn't had time to learn about the remarkable scientific work that was going on. I started thinking about Katarina Kreng, and how she wanted to destroy all the good work these scientists were doing! For what?

I checked my watch. It was five to ten. We had just over an hour to find door 218b. Leading us further along, the guide showed us into the control centre for the Atlas detector. She began explaining some of the science behind the experiments. Charlie was listening intently. She loved this! I, on the other hand, was scanning the crowd for signs of the weird man. I caught sight of him standing on the very edge of the group, nearest the monitoring equipment. He grinned at one of the scientists, seated at her desk, working quietly. As he turned, I noticed his small stained teeth. He was hideous. He made my skin creep! He must have had the same effect on the scientist, because she tried to smile politely, but didn't quite manage it. Her smile turned into a grimace and she excused herself from her desk. She left the room, holding her hand over her mouth; something had made her feel queasy.

I was a bit puzzled. Although the weird man was extremely unpleasant to look at, I couldn't imagine that the lady could have been so grossed out that she felt like throwing up! Then I remembered the smell. Maybe, up close and personal, his breath was bad enough to make someone ill. I couldn't pinpoint it, but something: a sixth sense had been awoken in me. There was something really wrong about this guy. I decided to watch him more closely, so I squeezed Charlie's hand to get her attention. She smiled and gazed into my eyes. She was still acting like the perfect girlfriend! I bent my head down to whisper in her ear, pretending to share a boyfriend/girlfriend "moment". She tilted her head so that her cheek was touching mine. Then she reached her hand up, resting it on my other cheek. The breath caught in my throat and my chest hurt. This was killing me. I didn't know if I could control myself anymore. I circled her head with my hand and pulled her to my chest, squeezing her tight to me, until the pain under my ribs had gone away. She pulled back and looked up into my eyes, confused. I know she felt something too because her cheeks were slightly flushed. I groaned softly, stepping back a pace. Maybe this acting thing wasn't such a good idea. Maybe it wasn't a good idea for Charlie and me to be together, at all. I couldn't concentrate when she was around.

And I really needed to concentrate right now!

29
The Unexpected

My phone started vibrating silently in my pocket. Gripping Charlie's hand in mine, I pulled her towards the door to the hallway. She was puzzled. A couple of other people from the group looked around at us curiously, as we left. One or two of them smiled. They probably thought we were going outside to "be alone" for a moment. Let them think that. It meant that our "act" was working and they wouldn't think anything of it when we left the group.

Once outside the door, I pulled my phone out of my pocket and hit the answer button. My cousin's face came on screen.

'Hey Cam…And, who's that?'

'Hi, I'm Mie,' said a beautiful blond girl with blue eyes and cherry lips.

'Oh, hi me… I mean…You,' I laughed, idiotically.

'Yeah, Mie knows Montreaux well. She's gonna take me to the Chateau du Chillon! Just letting you know that I'm OK.' he grinned.

'OK Cam, call me when you get there.'

'Bye Iago!' waved Mie into the camera.

'Bye Mie!' I grinned, as I hung up.

'Lucky Cam,' said Charlie.

'Phew, yeah – she's got it going on!' I replied.

Then I yelped in pain, as Charlie's sharp elbow almost pierced my ribs.

'What?' I asked, with a surprised tone.

'Aaaaggghh!' Charlie screamed quietly, stamping her foot on the floor.

'God, I hate you sometimes,' she hissed, heading back inside the door.

30
The Unthinkable

I slipped back inside the room behind her. An older couple smiled at us sweetly, probably remembering a time when they were young and had slipped off together. Boy, did they have the wrong end of the stick!

I quickly scanned the room for the weird guy. He was still by the desk of the nauseous scientist, who hadn't returned yet. He was sort of, leaning against the desk with his hands behind his back. I looked at his face; he seemed to be far away. Then I noticed the scientist's keyboard moving slowly towards him. He must have been dragging it! I continued to watch him as he turned slightly. I could only assume that he was typing something on the keyboard. What was he up to?

Unable to see the screen from where I was, I decided to wander around a bit, to try to get a better view. Charlie followed me with her eyes, though not with her feet. The moment had passed: Our boyfriend/girlfriend "act" was definitely OFF for now. She scowled at me. I just couldn't figure her out. She was just pretending to be my girlfriend, yet when I said I thought another girl was pretty, she got angry! Girls! How's a boy supposed to know what's going on?

I could just about see the screen, from my position behind a potted plant. The weird man's right hand tapped away furiously at the keyboard. I strained my eyes, trying desperately to make out what he was typing. I couldn't! I also couldn't possibly get any closer without him noticing me. What could I do? Then, like a coin in a slot, the penny dropped! I pulled my phone out of my pocket. It had a 10x optical zoom. I might not be able to read a screen from here but it could. I looked over at Charlie, hoping to share this eureka moment but she had her back to me. She seemed to be listening intently to the guide. Oh well, never mind. I zoomed and clicked. I carried on taking several photos. Then suddenly the weird man hit the return key, and walked away from the desk. I took one final photo!

31
The Unbelievable

I just stood there, staring at the photo. I couldn't think. I couldn't take my eyes off it. I couldn't call for help. I couldn't even move my head. The entire room had become silent and still. It was as if everything had been sucked into some kind of vortex. Then slowly, time began to speed up again. At first, it only ran at half normal-speed, so that when I turned my head, it seemed to take a long time. As I did so, I saw everyone else in the room moving really slowly. The guide raised her arm, pointing at something. It seemed to take a long time to reach its final position. All the visitors turned their faces upwards at half speed, following her movement. The sound track to this event was a low groaning noise, like an old-fashioned tape machine, its batteries running low.

Then in a flash, everything returned to normal. Charlie was by my side and the door was closing behind the weird man. 'You alright Iago?' asked Charlie. 'It's just - you don't look OK!' My mind raced. We had to follow him. I didn't have time to explain. 'Charlie, just trust me, we really need to go outside right now.' I looked a bit embarrassed and Charlie stared me out. I had upset her with my comments about Mie and I was worried that she wouldn't forgive me.

I didn't have time for any silly games but she looked so lovely, standing there in front of me, an angry little look on her face. I couldn't take any more. I took her face in my hands and I kissed her on the lips. As I pulled away, I looked deeply into her blue eyes.

'Come with me Char',' I pleaded. She bent her head, taking my hand and I followed her to the door.

'Don't do that again!' Charlie spat, as soon as the door closed behind us. I was confused; I thought she liked it! Obviously, I was wrong. Maybe I was just imagining things. I was about to ask her what the hell was going on, when she suddenly circled her arms around my waist and laughed. Had she been just teasing me? I looked down at her face and then I realised that she was acting again. She was still smiling, but through gritted teeth she whispered, 'He's coming this way. Kiss me!'

I wasn't going to argue with her about that. I bent my head to kiss her. This time Charlie's kiss was mechanical - like something you see in a film. I was disappointed, but I had a role to play so I kissed her back and ran my hand through her hair.

His smell grew stronger as he approached us, and instinct made me turn my back to him. Charlie was now shielded from his horrible presence. But she could still just see him over my shoulder. Charlie lowered her head and I let my lips settle softly on her silky hair. Then she looked up. I could see the look of horror in her eyes as he walked past. He was still twittering to himself and sniggering about something. He didn't pay any attention to us, whatsoever. Our act seemed to be working.

As soon as he had passed, Charlie unravelled her arms from around my waist and I released her. She stood back against the wall, her eyes cast down to the floor. She looked uncomfortable.

I felt really confused, but now was definitely not the time for feelings. I had to tell her about the weird man. Pulling my phone out, I opened the photo. I didn't say a word, just showed her the screen. She frowned, as she tried to work out what she was looking at. Then gasped as she realised what she was seeing.

'Iago, is that what I think it is? I mean, where did you get this picture? I mean... when did you take this?' She looked at me, confused.

'I took it about two minutes ago, in the control room. It's a photo of the screen that lady was working at – you know, the one who left, looking ill! The weird stinky man must have logged into the system and started it...'

'But Iago... it's a countdown!'

'I know!'

'But a countdown to what?'

'I have no idea!'

'Well we'd better find out!'

'We need to find that man!'

'Shouldn't be too difficult!' she said, sniffing.

Despite our situation - we both laughed.

32
The Ohmigod

We crept cautiously up to the door the stinky man had just closed. I peeped through the glass panel - no sign of him! Pushing open the hinged door, we quietly stepped through. I flinched as the door swung squeakily behind us. I looked at Charlie and she frowned. 'Not fair!' I thought to myself. It wasn't my fault that it was a squeaky door.

We were in a corridor.

Charlie kept tight to the wall, as she cautiously crept along to the corner. She popped her head around it, and quickly jumped back. Pointing her finger, she mouthed, 'He's there!' I crept forward to join her. Sticking my head briefly around the corner, I saw the man walking towards some more doors at the end of the short corridor. We waited until we heard the doors open and swing closed behind him. Then, after checking once again, we left the safety of our hiding place and darted straight for the doors he had just gone through. We couldn't afford to lose him now!

We entered a small laboratory of some sort. Standing perfectly still with my back to the door, I motioned to Charlie to crouch down. We were communicating like a special ops team now. I didn't know the correct hand signals, but it felt good. I pointed to my eyes with both my fingers and then pointed to the corner on my right. Charlie snickered. I glared! Then I saw the funny side; maybe I should leave out the SAS hand signals. I probably looked a bit of a prat!

I crept forward on my knees. Charlie stayed by the door. Taking a deep breath, I stuck my head around the corner. The weird man was sitting at a computer, with his back to me. He was blocking the screen, so I couldn't see what he was doing. Inching slowly forward, I reached the cover of a desk. Scanning the room, I decided that I would have to crawl from desk to desk to get a decent view. I stretched out flat on my stomach and crawled forward. Progress was slow. It's actually quite hard to drag yourself forwards on your elbows!

Finally, reaching the cover of the closest desk, I peeked carefully round it. I could see the screen now but nothing made any sense to me. All I could see were sequences of numbers - all that crawling for nothing! I pulled back behind the desk. Something moving to my right caught my attention; it was Charlie. She was jumping up and down, waving her arms. Lunatic!

'What?' I mouthed, narrowing my eyes. I was not impressed with her behaviour. Was she trying to get caught? Then a noise on the other side of the desk made me jump. There were no other people in this room and, unless it was a very large lab-rat, I could only think of one person it could be. In either case, I didn't want to stick around. There was no point in secrecy now. He either knew about me already, or was going to find out in about one second. I stood up suddenly and ran!

Grabbing a stunned Charlie on the way past, I dove through the lab doors. As the doors swung shut behind us, I heard a dull thud. The spring-hinged door swung open again and to my horror, there, in the door, was what looked like a bullet hole!

'Is that...?' began Charlie. I just looked at her, my mouth open in shock. 'Is it, Iago?' she said again, her voice rising. 'We're not going to stick around to find out!' I said, trying to sound heroic. I pulled her up by her elbow. She looked frightened but suddenly her "fight or flight instinct" kicked in. She bolted!

Charlie was through the next set of doors before I'd even started running. She stopped on the other side to wait for me. 'Which way, Iago?' she asked, as soon as I had joined her. 'We've got to lead him away from the public areas,' I replied. 'He's got a gun. He has just shot at us. He clearly isn't too worried about "collateral damage".' I cringed as that last bit replayed in my head - collateral damage - I really needed to stop watching action movies! Charlie rolled her eyes at me. Yeah, she definitely heard it! God, how uncool was I now?

Luckily, or unluckily, (I never got chance to work it out), the small glass pane in the double doors shattered and tiny bits landed in Charlie's hair. As she turned to look back at the door, the splinters sparkled in the overhead lights. She looked like a sparkly Christmas angel. I shook my head - what a weird thought to have at a time like this. I grabbed her hand. This weird guy was serious. He seemed to be actually trying to shoot us. I didn't have time to think, I just ran!

The corridor to our left ended with a sharp right corner. It was about thirty metres long. There was no way we could make it to the end before the weird guy got off another shot. I tried a door handle as I passed; it was locked. Seeing what I was doing, Charlie tried one on her side of the corridor. She shook her head.

Without breaking my stride, I swivelled my head round to look for our attacker. He stood with his feet planted as he raised his weapon in both hands. Charlie screamed! I dived on top of her and we crashed to the ground. There was a small spray of plaster as the bullet hit the back wall. From the height of the bullet hole, it looked like the weird guy was aiming for my body. My body! Now it was my turn to scream! Scrambling to my feet, I pulled Charlie towards the corner. Another spray of plaster greeted us as we neared the bend. Raising her hand to cover her eyes, Charlie was first around the corner. I followed her as our attacker fired another bullet, this time hitting the corner where my head had just passed.

'Iago!' Charlie cried, grabbing my hand. Our footsteps thundered down the corridor as our eyes desperately searched for an escape route. There were doors on either side but could we risk stopping at every door to try it? Our attacker was nowhere in sight, but I was sure that he wasn't going to give up now. As we raced down the corridor, I could see that it ended in a wall of glass. The glass seemed to be green. But it wasn't solid green. It seemed to flicker, and the shade of green seemed to change constantly. My ears pricked up – there was a shuffling noise behind me. I wheeled around to see the weird guy rounding the bend. He wasn't moving as fast as Charlie and I, but then again - he didn't need to.

He had a gun!

33
The Oasis

The wall of glass shattered into a million pieces in front of us, as the bullet sped between us. Now I could see that, what I had thought was green glass, was actually trees! It seemed to be some kind of indoor courtyard, filled with bushes and small trees. I couldn't make out the other side of this indoor garden, so it must have been quite large. As we ran through the shattered pane of glass, I looked up. I could see blue sky through a huge skylight high above, and it seemed that every floor overlooked this green oasis. There were people standing by the windows on the second floor, deep in conversation. They didn't seem to have noticed the sound of the bullet, or seen the pane of glass shatter.

I pulled Charlie around behind a bush. This wouldn't offer us any protection against bullets, but at least he couldn't see us. We took a second to catch our breath. We could hear his dreadful footsteps getting closer. He slowed - he didn't need to run now... we were trapped. We were in an enclosed space and he had control of the only exit. All he had to do was stay there and wait for us to come to him!

But he didn't!

Then, I realised that, of course, he couldn't. He had set

off some kind of timer. We had disturbed him in the lab. He needed to finish us off and get back to his work. He didn't have time to chase us around this indoor oasis.

I signalled to Charlie. We began backing slowly away from his position.

'You can't hope to get out of here alive, surely?' came the man's nasal voice from dead ahead. 'I mean. Be realistic. You don't really expect to get past an armed man...do you?' He sniggered and guffawed to himself. He was revolting, even when you couldn't see him. I looked at Charlie. She wrinkled her nose. She felt it too. We continued creeping carefully away from him. Then a thought occurred to me: Maintenance! There must be a gardener to take care of the greenery. He'd need access. There must be a way out!

Instead of heading for the centre, where the greenery would give us better cover, I decided to scope out the glass walls for a door. Charlie tugged my sleeve and looked at me, puzzled. I couldn't take a chance on even whispering my idea to her. I just put my hand gently on her face, and smiled. I hoped that she understood that I would protect her.

We crept noiselessly along the outer edge of the bushes. Since the weird guy had gone towards the middle of the garden, we kept our eyes focussed there.

So, it took us completely by surprise!

The gardener, pruning shears in hand, swung the door open right behind us. It was amazing. The door looked exactly like all the other panes of glass. There were no markings or handle on it. We would never have spotted it. The opening mechanism must have been triggered automatically by the man's security badge. The poor man looked totally shocked. His eyes widened as he tried to take in what he saw. 'Qu'est ce que vous faites ici?' he asked in heavily accented French. I didn't really need to translate. He had asked what anyone would - 'What are you doing here?'

Charlie held her finger to her lips and waved him down. She whispered, 'Il y a un homme dangereux ici!' Her French wasn't much better than mine, but she always gave things a go! The man stayed still and listened. He could hear the weird guy calling to us, 'Come out, come out, wherever you are?'

Although the gardener had no idea how dangerous our attacker was, he clearly didn't like to see us in danger. 'Venez!' he whispered. Charlie looked at his outstretched hand and then at me. 'You go!' I whispered. 'I will try to lead him away from you.' 'No Iago,' she almost cried, 'he's too dangerous!'

'Look Charlie,' I replied calmly, 'you have to get to that door by 11am, otherwise everything is lost. We're never going to make it with this guy following us. We've got to split up! You are, by far, the better runner. You need to go now. I'll stay in touch and as soon as I can, I will come and help. OK?' Although she didn't want to accept it, she knew I was right. She wrapped her arms tightly around my neck and I hugged her in reply. When she pulled back, I could see one shiny tear sliding slowly down her cheek.

Then she backed away and took the gardener's hand. He looked at me with a puzzled expression as I began to move quickly away from them and the door. Then they were gone! I slipped around a small palm tree trunk and stood with my back pressed tightly against it. I needed to be still and listen for a moment.

I wasn't expecting it.

Something came from my left and hit me with lightening speed. I heard the crunch before I felt the pain. Then I felt something warm trickling down my cheek, before everything went black.

34

The Outside

I woke up in a small dimly lit space. Looking around, I could see nobody else in the room. I tried to stand up, but realised that I was attached to something. My head throbbed and my eyes blurred, as I twisted around to see what was holding me down. When my vision cleared, I saw that my wrists were bound to a heating pipe by a large knot. Instinct made me test the knot, by trying to pull my hands apart. No go! Then I tested the heating pipe, by leaning my bodyweight away from it. It didn't give at all. It didn't even creak. It was solid. Whoever had trussed me up had done a good job!

My phone vibrated in my shirt pocket. Looking down at my shirt, I had mixed feelings. Firstly, I was relieved that whoever had left me here had not taken my phone. And secondly, I was annoyed that I was not able to answer it. I was left guessing as to who was calling me. This couldn't be happening.

Scanning the room, I desperately tried to figure out where I was, but the only light in the room came from underneath the door. It seemed to me that I was in a small office at the end of a larger space. There was a hum of equipment outside. That didn't help narrow it down -

equipment hums everywhere! I had to assume that I was still inside CERN, so it was likely that the next room was some sort of lab, or control centre. My phone rang again. I had to find a way of answering it. Someone must need my help. Although to be honest, I couldn't offer much help, being tied up to a heating pipe and all!

Shuffling to my feet, I stood with my back to the heating duct. Straightening my legs, I bent my body forward. Not being that flexible it took a few tries, but finally I managed to lean my body forward just enough so that my phone slipped out of my shirt pocket.

I winced as it landed with a crack on the tile floor. Nervously stretching out my foot, I slid the phone carefully towards me. To my relief, it seemed to be perfectly fine. I just hoped it still worked!

There was still the problem of how to operate it with both my hands behind my back. I had no choice! I quickly shook off my shoe, and using my other foot tugged off my sock - not an easy thing to do! I shuffled the phone round on the floor until I got it into a position where I could use my big toe. It was painfully slow but finally I managed to click on the video message I had received. It was from Cam. My heart sank. Although I was happy to hear from my cousin, I thought it might be Charlie. Now I began to worry again, about what had happened to her. I hoped she had made it to the door – everything depended on that!

I opened the MP4 file and Cam began speaking…

'Iago – you OK? Don't know why you're not answering but if you get this, I need your help. I am at the Chateau de Chillon. We joined the tour group. I don't know if I told you this, but I googled and found out that Lord Byron wrote a poem about somebody called Francois Bonivard, who was held prisoner here from 1532 to 1536. We are in the room where he was held, but I can't see anything. Cam out!'

The file ended. I tried to remember the second line of the riddle that Katarina Kreng had set us - something about Lord Byron's prisoner and a lake. But Cam already knew all this. Cam was at Lake Geneva. The Chateau was on the lake. What other information did he need? There was no other information in that riddle. Maybe it was a wild goose chase. Maybe she thought that we would all go looking for my dad. With us out of the picture, she could focus on her evil plan. My blood boiled. She underestimated us. We were strong together, but each one of us of could work alone, so long as we knew that we all had each other's backs covered! I took a deep breath and focussed. Cam needed my help now. I recalled the line from the riddle, word for word – "where Byron's "prisoner" had a nice view of the lake…" That was it! I scrolled through my options as best as I could, with my big toe, and finally hit reply.

Cam answered instantly.

'Where have you been Iago?'

'A bit tied up Cam!' I grinned, but decided not to tell him my story.

'Cam, is there a window in that room?'

'Yeah, but it's a small one and quite high up. This was a prison cell, remember!'

'You need to get to it. The riddle mentions the "view" of the lake. I think that whatever your next clue is, you can only see it from that window!'

'The room is pretty full right now. I'll have to wait until the tour moves on. Get back to you later, Cuz!'

And then he was gone. All of a sudden, I felt alone and, if I was honest, a little bit scared!

35
The Opening

Then the phone rang again – maybe I wasn't so all alone! Clumsily, I hit the answer button with my toe. It was Charlie.

'Oh Iago, I'm so glad to see you. Listen, I'm near the door. It's five to eleven by my watch. The problem is that there are CCTV cameras on every door. I can't just hang around by the door waiting for it to unlock – I'll be spotted. You've got to do something!'

'Relax Charlie. Stay where you are. I'll see what I can do!'

'By the way, where are you Iago?' she asked suspiciously.

'Why is it so dark? I can barely see your face. Turn on some lights, for heaven's sake!'

'Emm…I'm not able to do that, just at the minute.' I hoped I didn't let too much slip – I didn't want to worry her.

'I'll get back to you in one minute – OK?'

I hit "end call".

Renny answered on the first beep or buzz or whatever he had his phone set to do. He carried on typing on his laptop and only glanced at his screen to say,

'Hey Iago!'

'Renny, we need to access the CCTV screen at the door. Charlie will be spotted if she hangs around too long.

'Hang on,' replied Renny, as he typed, 'OK...I can create a 30 second loop and replay it so that the security guards don't see her.'

'How long do you need?' I asked, checking the time on my screen. It was three minutes to eleven.

'About two minutes,' he muttered.

'It had better not take any longer, Renny!' I could see him turn his head to look at his watch. 'Yikes!' he shrieked when he saw what I meant. 'I'm on it!'

'Let me know!' I smiled and switched off.

I leaned my head back against the heating pipe and let out a long sigh. The gnawing feeling in the pit of my stomach felt more like bats than butterflies. I checked my watch again: eleven fifty eight... Two minutes to go!

My phone beeped again. It was Charlie. I flicked it on.

'Any news?' she whispered.

'Renny's working on it, but it will be tight!' I said, trying to sound upbeat.

'Like, how tight?' she asked.

'Very!' I replied.

'OK Iago – I'm waiting...' she said softly.

And her face disappeared. I missed her instantly!

Then my phone beeped once again. This time it was Renny. Nervously I checked the time – eleven fifty nine!

'Tell me it's a go, Renny,' I snapped.

'Not yet mate, sorry!' he replied.

'But Renny...' I hissed.

'Remember they said the door would be open for five minutes,' he said.

I sighed as I remembered. Then I looked directly at my

cousin, 'Get it done!' I growled, punching the end call button with my toe. A sharp pain shot up my foot and barely stifling a squeal, I reminded myself to calm down.

I got back to Charlie and told her to wait. The minutes dragged past.

11.01

11.02

11.03

Still no word from Renny.

I was about to order Charlie to go to the door and risk being spotted. We could not fail to get through the door. On the other hand, making it through the door meant nothing if she got picked up on the other side!

11.04 – I put my big toe to the screen. It hovered…

Then the call came!

'Go…go…go!' shouted Renny, as I answered. I relayed the message to Charlie as quick as I could, and I could hear her running. I couldn't see much except the floor of the corridor. By my clock, she had twenty seconds left. She had at least one hundred metres to run. I didn't know if even she could make it! I couldn't look!

Charlie's phone clattered against something. I tried to make out what was going on! I could only see white. The phone was pressed against something.

I checked the time again: five… four… three… two… one…

I held my breath…

36
The Oscar

Then I heard a click. Was this good news or bad? The click could be Charlie opening the door or it could be the door locking itself, as the hackers said it would.

I waited…and exhaled.

Then Charlie's face came on screen. Her cheeks were bright red and she was desperately trying to catch her breath. She heaved in and out a few times. My nerves were screaming. Finally, she straightened up…

'I made it,' she grinned, and I almost passed out with relief.

'You need to get moving Charl,' I smiled down at her face in my screen.

'Again Iago, where ARE you? Your face looks weird, and like I said - turn on some lights!'

'I'm kinda stuck here at the moment' I replied, suddenly feeling weak.

'What do you mean stuck?' Charlie snapped back.

Now I felt even worse. I was going to have to confess to being kidnapped!

'Well, he captured me and now I'm in a closet, attached to a heating duct!'

'Well, you'd better find a way to uncapture yourself,

Iago. We NEED you!'

I heard a muffled sound from the other side of the door. Mustn't let him know where Charlie's heading.

'Gotta go Charl. Just RUN!' I whispered, stabbing at my phone with my toe to end the call.

I slid my phone under the shelf to my left. I hadn't had time to set the "silent ring", so I hoped the gang didn't need me for a while! Getting my sock and shoe on in time was another matter. I kicked my sock as far away as I could. It landed just behind the door. I hoped he wouldn't notice it. I just about got my toes into my shoe, when the door burst open. I froze. He still had a gun and just because he hadn't killed me yet, it didn't mean he wouldn't!

Again, the foul smell that filled the small room was unbelievable. I almost gagged as he grinned at me slowly. His smile showed a row of front teeth that ranged from yellow to dark orange. The urge to close my eyes was strong. I really tried hard to keep my face blank - mustn't give him any reason to be angry with me!

'What am I to do with you?' he asked. His voice surprised me. I was expecting a voice that matched the face. In fact, the voice and the face seemed strangely at odds with each other. While the face was...well, disgusting, the voice was actually very soft and cultured.

The surprise must have shown on my face because he snapped, 'What did you expect: the elephant man?'

I was confused. I didn't know what he was talking about but there was no way I was going to ask him.

He raised his gun. I shrank back in horror, trying to make myself as small as possible. He grinned wickedly at my fear. 'Maybe, I'll just leave you here! I've almost finished my part – now we just have to wait and see. I'm sure that someone will find you here… eventually!

Then he started mumbling to himself again. It was like looking at a split personality. One of his faces grinned, as an idea seemed to come to him then, the grumpy face took over as he pooh-poohed his own idea.

'On second thoughts,' he said, suddenly dashing towards me.

Pushing me over, he untied my wrists. I shook my hands in front of me, as the blood surged back painfully through my veins.

'Get up!' he ordered.

Flicking my eyes nervously to where my phone lay under the shelf, I shuffled to my knees. What was I going to do? I couldn't leave it behind. I would be no use to the others. They needed to talk to me. Someone needed to coordinate the whole thing. I had to get it.

Lifting my right leg, I placed my foot in front of me and started to stand up. Then, groaning with cramp, I lurched sideways, crashing into the shelf beside me. Sliding back down to the floor, I carried on groaning. In a flash, I had slipped my hand under the shelf and dragged my phone to my side. Gripping it carefully in my palm, I secreted it into the side pocket of my jeans, while holding my leg and rolling from side to side. 'Ah, ah, ah…cramp!' I said, looking up at the man. A look of concern flashed across his face and he surprised me by bending down beside me. Then, taking my calf between his hands, he began massaging it.

'Oh…that's better!' I said, watching his face intently. He had a faraway look in his eyes and a certain softness made his ugly face seem… sweet.

Then, like a switch being flicked, his eyes froze over

and he dragged me to my feet. Pushing me out the door in front of him, he ran to a desk and picked up a laptop. I just caught a glimpse of the screen before he snapped it closed. It was the clock. We were still on a countdown. Time was not on my side – the clock read 00:49. Whatever we were going to do, we had only forty-nine minutes to do it.

37
The Observation

Looking at my watch nervously, I tried to calculate whether Charlie could possibly search ten kilometres in forty-nine minutes. After a couple of minutes of brain-pain mental arithmetic, I gave up. Although I wasn't bad at maths, I wasn't that good either. I liked to think I had other qualities! I was worried though. It still seemed like a lot of running to me!

My captor distracted me from my thought-stream by kicking something, and I was almost grateful. There was no use in panicking now. Charlie would do whatever she could. In the meantime, I realised that I didn't have a back-up plan. If, for some reason, Charlie was not able to find the fail-safe or, if Renny couldn't get his GeekGrid together in time or, if the girls couldn't patch the signal through the computer centre, we were stuffed! That was a lot of "ifs". I really needed some feedback from the gang. Then my phone pinged, just once!

Nervously, I looked up towards my captor. He didn't seem to have noticed it. I hadn't had time to set the silent ring but luckily I don't do ringtones! There was no way I could answer right now; I just hoped that whoever it was could wait!

'Move it!' came a shout from across the room. Startled, I jumped to attention. Standing, holding the door open with his foot, he waved the gun back and forth. I took this to mean that I was to go through. Just to the left was a sign for the emergency stairs. He lifted the security bar and the light above started flashing. He didn't seem to notice, or didn't care. Looking back over his shoulder and seeing the question in my eyes he grinned, 'All be over by the time they find me…!' Then he skipped off down the stairs, like a giddy four year old.

After heading down several flights of stairs, he threw open one of the emergency doors. Holding it open, he peeped through, checking up and down the corridor. I guessed that no one was coming, since he shoved me through it a second later. Squeezing my arm, he pushed me along the corridor. He seemed nervous now, his head flicking left to right with every step. We turned a corner. Just ahead of us, a hanging sign read "Atlas – Maintenance shaft". I tried to guess what he was planning. I couldn't begin to imagine.

Getting through the access doors to the maintenance shaft was easy. He had some kind of security card. He just inserted it into the slot and the door opened automatically. Once through the doors, he pushed me towards a small hatch in the wall at the far side of the corridor. 'Turn it!' he barked, flipping open his laptop. He seemed to be checking the time. 'He needs to be somewhere!' I thought. I turned the handle and the hatch's mechanical lock sprung back. At first, I thought that it was strange to have an old-fashioned mechanical lock. Then I realised that if they had electronic locks and the complex lost power for any reason, the engineers wouldn't be able to get in.

Slamming his laptop shut with a bang that surprised me, he muttered 'Get in!' His hand was in his pocket and he, sort of, waved it at me. 'Gun!' I remembered and turned to climb through the hatch. I stepped through onto a small metal ledge, about one foot wide. A waist-height safety bar surrounded it. To my left, I saw a ladder. It was one of those safety ladders with the metal bars every few feet. Looking down I could see a ledge, just like the one I was on, below me. All I could see past that was the ladder descending into the darkness. A shiver went down my spine.

The weird guy poked me and I shuffled nervously to the side. 'Down,' he muttered, joining me on the small ledge. Taking a deep breath, I stepped onto the first rung. That went OK. I started climbing down. Strange thoughts were running through my head. I remembered a day on the beach with my dog, both of us just running into and back out of the water. I was quite young then and I remembered the joy of chasing waves. I hadn't done that in a long time. Suddenly, it was the only thing in the world I wanted to do. I tilted my head to look up at the vile man above me. Was he part of the evil plan to annihilate the world? He had to be! Why else would he have followed Charlie and me? Who did these people think they were? No human being has the right to end the world, no matter what kind of mess we've made of it.

We had moved past the lower ledge and were heading into the darkness. I had to slow down, as it was getting harder to see the next rung on the ladder. After a while, I couldn't see them at all. I had to feel below me for each one. Finally, my foot hit something solid. I sighed with relief as I stood, my two feet now firmly on the floor.

38
The Obvious

The weird guy pushed me backwards as soon as he reached the floor. 'Vile and rude!' I thought, stumbling, while he fished around for something near the base of the ladder. 'Got it!' he said. Then a strong beam of light shone down the dark tunnel. The sides of the tunnel were curved metal, and the torch's full beam lit up the whole place. As the weird guy shuffled forward, I followed; there wasn't much point in trying to escape. I would only get about three rungs up the ladder before he shot me. And besides, I was beginning to think that I needed to be with him. I needed to figure out exactly what was going on!

The low ceiling of the metal tunnel caused me to stoop slightly. As we moved forward through the tunnel, darkness closed in behind me. It felt solid, like a door shutting, locking me in. My nerves jangled but I carried on walking, telling myself all the while that this was just a dark tunnel. There was nothing here, except me... *and* the maniac with the gun.

Then a squeaking noise came from right behind me. I stopped, for just a second, forcing myself to turn my head around and face the darkness. Then I saw it - scuttling towards me. I could only just make it out in the fading light. My senses dimmed as I realised that it could only be one thing… a rat!

Clamping my hand over my mouth, I ran forward. The weird guy was now quite far ahead. He didn't seem to notice that I had fallen behind. Maybe he didn't care! Maybe he knew that I would rather stay with him than be left in this rat-infested tunnel alone… He wasn't wrong!

I caught up with him just as he reached another hatch. He was already trying to turn the handle, whilst not dropping his precious laptop.

'Here, let me!' I smiled, stepping past him. I was very keen to be out of the tunnel; anywhere had to be better than here! Yanking the handle down hard, I pushed the hatch open. The weird man pushed past me.

Dropping his laptop carefully to the ground on the other side, he followed it. His feet were barely through the hatch when I launched myself through it, landing in a heap beside him. Quickly scuttling to my feet, I smiled at him. I knew I looked a bit too happy for someone in my position. But I was glad to be out of that tunnel!

'Another corridor!' I thought to myself as I looked around. The weird guy was checking his countdown again. Then he raced towards a door. I followed him through it. We were in some kind of control room. Not THE control room but it definitely controlled something. The weird guy was plugging his laptop into a network. This must be his control room. He must have set this up a long time ago! He clearly had some kind of control over the LHC from here. But this meant that he must have worked for CERN! But, if he worked here, what would make him want to destroy the earth?

He must have read the question on my mind because he

turned to me and laughed.

'I suppose I should put you out of your misery! After all, you're never going to get the chance to tell anyone about it. It will be our little secret!' He tapped the side of his nose and winked.

'You see, I've worked for the good of science most of my life. And where's it ever got me? Nowhere! While others got the applause, the glory…the girl…!' He paused here and screwed up his face in anger, 'I got nothing!' He walked up and down a couple of times, grinning horribly one minute, then looking sad and wistful the next.

'Well, all that's changed! Now I will be the one getting something!' His voice was starting to rise and as it did, he raised his arms in the air. 'In fact, I am getting more money than you can possibly imagine. With this much money I can have it all!'

So *this* was all about money? I couldn't believe what I was hearing.

'But who would give you money to destroy the world?' I asked sheepishly. It felt like a stupid question, but I couldn't think of one person who would be better off if the world suddenly disappeared.

'Aha… good question!' he replied, raising his finger in the air. 'Let me explain.' Scrolling through his laptop's menu, he opened up a PowerPoint file. A second later, the file started playing. The first image that came up was of sacks of coffee beans. A question floated across the screen from left to right,

'How much is this worth?'

The text carried on moving across the screen, flipped over, then started running back in the opposite direction. The image changed to oil barrels, then chocolate bars, then

135

bars of gold, then milk bottles. All the time the text chased across the screen, backwards and forwards, backwards and forwards. The screen went black and after a few seconds, text started coming up from the bottom of the screen. It read:

IF

WE

CONTROL IT...

An image began to form on the screen - first one bag, and then another appeared. Each bag with a dollar sign on it, gold coins spilling out the top. A line of red text flashed in the centre of the screen.

...IT'S PRICELESS!

The text changed colour, flashed a few times, and finally disappeared. After a second, a logo flashed up on screen. A company logo - I recognised it. It was a fat king sitting on a throne, outlined in gold. It was the logo for KING UNITED AGGREGATES - a company who were known for chasing profit, no matter what. They didn't pretend to be interested in ethical businesses. They didn't pretend to believe in renewable energy sources. They didn't care that their products were made by children, being paid pennies for working fifteen hours a day. They didn't care about the destruction of the rainforests, the oceans, the Antarctic, or the planet. As long as they made as much money as they could for themselves, they didn't care what harm they caused.

After the presentation ended, I just stood there, thinking. No matter which way I looked at it, I still couldn't see how even King-UA could benefit if the world ended.

Then it dawned on me. Swivelling round to face my captor, I said, 'You're not going to destroy the world, are you?'

'Ahhhhhhh… clever boy!' replied the weird man, smirking. 'You're right - what would be the point in that? No, no… we are just going to take it to the edge. Let's see what they are willing to give us then. Imagine their surprise!' Here, he bowed low, putting on a theatrical voice, "Your choice, Mr Presidents and Mr Prime Ministers and you other world leaders… give us total control of coal, oil, gas, metals, energy supply, cotton, coffee and, not forgetting - chocolate, or face… annihilation!" Somehow, I think they'll give in. Don't you?' he said, swivelling on his heel. 'Then WE will decide how much you pay to run your car, heat your home, buy a new mobile phone and even…how much you pay for your favourite chocolate bar!'

Again, he grinned at me as he drilled the message home. He rubbed his hands together greedily, chuckling to himself. I tried to take in everything he had just told me.

Then his computer screen flashed with an incoming video call. He turned to it, leaving me alone to think about his terrible plans - *one company owning all of the world's resources!* That kind of power should never be in the hands of one company, especially not one a vile as King-UA!

My shocked eyes were suddenly drawn to the screen as the ugly face of Katarina Kreng filled the screen.

'Report!' snapped the weird man, without looking up at the screen.

'Oh Hali…stop trying to sound bossy. It doesn't suit you!' she replied, laughing.

'Hali?' I thought. 'Where have I heard that name before?'

It took a long time and my brain hurt. I had to search through the filing cabinet in my head. Trouble was - I wasn't a very good secretary. Normally I filed everything under M, for Miscellaneous or O, for Other. The problem with that was that those files ended up being pretty fat!

But I knew that I'd heard the name recently. Suddenly Uncle Jonas's face swam before me. I could see his lips moving. Now I remembered – Hali had been an old friend and co-worker of Uncle Jonas! Could the two-headed monster of greed and envy have turned a one-time friend into a madman?

39
The Opposite

My phone pinged again. I looked up cautiously. Hali was focusing on the screen. Stepping back a few paces, I gingerly reached for my side pocket. I fumbled for the phone while turning my body slightly. Holding my phone up to waist height, I put my Bluetooth earpiece in.

'Cam?' I whispered.

'Why you whispering, Iago?'

'Never mind!' I hissed. 'What did you find out?'

'Well, you were right - the view from the window. On the hillside, across the lake was a flag - A CERN flag!'

'That's got to be it then!'

'Yeah, we're on our way now.'

'Is Mie still with you?'

'Yeah!' smiled Cam, happily. The camera swirled round and Mie's pretty face filled the screen. She grinned and waved.

'Lucky Cam!' I whispered to him.

'Yeah, for once,' he replied. 'Get back to you soon! Cam out!'

40
The Overload

The sight of Cam with Mie made me miss Charlie suddenly. A pang hit my stomach as I thought of her. I wanted to make sure she was OK, but I couldn't risk another call right now. As I turned back towards the screen, although I couldn't see Katarina Kreng's ugly face, I could hear her horrid voice. Her oversized front teeth made her spit every time she came to an s, or a p sound. I was glad I wasn't that webcam. Creeping forward a few steps, I tried to hear her more clearly.

'Well, the little geese are on the chase. They should be reaching clue number two anytime now. I don't think they will riddle their little feathers out of this one,' she giggled at her own joke. Then she carried on, 'but even if they do, it will probably be too late. The train leaves in twenty-five minutes. Then it's just a matter of time before "pouff"!' I just caught sight of her throwing her arms up in the air.

I was stuck to the floor with horror. My mouth hung open but my brain was totally frozen. Was she talking about my dad? What did she mean by "pouff"? Then the image started forming in my mind - my dad and a bomb. My dad and a bomb…

My dad and a BOMB!

My senses screamed back to reality. I wanted to run to the screen and smash it into a billion tiny pieces, but that wouldn't help! I wanted to attack Hali but there was no point. Not now that I knew, that there were two of them. They both had to be stopped.

Then Hali turned to look at me over his shoulder. 'There is just one small problem with your wild goose chase, Katarina,' he growled. 'There were a few more geese than you anticipated, and some of the geese weren't in the mood for a treasure hunt!' He reached out and grabbed me by the sleeve, tugging me forward, until I stood in front of her ugly face.

'Mmmmm, what a pretty little gosling!' she jeered and suddenly, I felt jittery, as if ants were crawling all over me.

'He had a little girlfriend,' Hali joined in the jeering, 'but she got away.'

'What do you mean she got away?' snapped Katarina. 'We can't have some child running around, messing things up! Go and find her!'

'Bu…bu... but… the timer. Who is going to stop the annihilation?' Hali stammered, his eyes flashing worriedly.

'Once you set it up, I can monitor it from here,' answered Katarina calmly. Then, glaring at Hali, she moved closer to her webcam.

'Well I can't find her from here, can I? I knew I should have come there straightaway. I knew you couldn't handle it on your own.' She was getting angry now and Hali was shaking slightly. 'Transfer the controls to me and GO FIND THAT GIRL!' She was almost screaming by the end of the sentence.

Hali jumped to it. He started typing furiously, mumbling to himself all the while. After a few moments of huffing and puffing, he lifted his head. Turning towards me, he raised his gun. Fear tore through me, as I froze on the spot. 'Come and help me find your little girlfriend, then,' he said waving the gun towards the door. I had just started to move slowly to my left when Katarina cried out, 'No. The gosling stays!'

'But why?' asked Hali pathetically, turning back to face her.

'I can keep an eye on him from here. I don't want to take a chance on him escaping from you too. It's bad enough that we have one little loose goose running around!'

Obviously furious at the way she spoke to him, Hali gripped my arm tightly.

'Owwww,' I yelped in pain.

'Oh, sorry,' he replied gently, his face changing from fury to pity. I couldn't figure him out. He really was a Jekyll and Hyde creature. Maybe years of defeat and lack of achievement did that to a person. Despite his cruelty, I began to feel sorry for him...

So, I was tied to another heating duct, and Hali raced out the door.

'That man is such a fool,' grinned Katarina, sitting back in her chair. 'I never would have dreamt of using him, except that I needed someone on the inside!'

I looked nervously at the screen. Was she talking to me? Why was she telling me this? I didn't like where this was going. I turned my head slightly away from her horrible face. But that didn't stop her.

'That poor fool thinks that I'm interested in money! I only needed him and his little 'King Ag' buddies to gain access to the LHC, but now I have the controls!' She threw her head back and laughed like a maniac. Then she stopped suddenly, staring straight into her webcam. 'Now, my little gosling, do you know what day it is today?'

I knew that it was a Friday, but I shook my head, knowing that she wasn't looking for an answer from me.

'Today, she continued grandly, 'is the day we get to see what happens… after the end of the world…'

41
The Other Side

I sat there in stunned silence for I don't know how long. The nothingness just ticked in my ears. I didn't blink. I didn't swallow. I don't think I even breathed.

Then I heard my own voice feebly stuttering, 'What happens after the end of the world? What do you mean *AFTER* the end of the world? The end of the world is, "the end of the world" surely. I mean, there is NO "after the end of the world"!'

I just stood there, staring at her image on the screen. I was frightened of this woman - more frightened of her than I had been of Hali. He was greedy and he could be mean, but she was MAD!

She laughed at me. 'Oh, my little gosling,' she carried on and the hairs on my neck stood up. The gosling thing was starting to annoy me. 'Imagine, standing on the edge of a black hole and watching everything melt into its liquid loveliness. Imagine seeing time stretching back and forwards in shimmering shafts across the universe. Imagine being reborn on the other side. It's all possible, you know. *You just have to believe!*'

I gasped! I didn't know whether I should believe what my ears were hearing - "You just have to believe..." Now

I knew she was insane! I tried to go over everything in my mind. From what I understood, Katarina had planned everything. She had convinced Hali and his friends at King United Aggregates that she could bring the world to the brink of annihilation and then stop it. In their greed, they went along with her plan. From their point of view, it was a win-win situation. They could use this to persuade governments around the world to give them control of all of the world's resources. To these greedy people this meant absolute power and wealth. But, they had not counted on one thing; Katarina Kreng was mad - stone cold, stark raving MAD! She had no intention of stopping the annihilation. She was going to go all the way. She would destroy the entire world!

I shivered as I realised that only one thing could stop her - US! Our plan was all that stood between her and the end of the world. The only problem was - it was a very loose plan with a lot of moving parts. If just one of those moving parts broke down, if any one of us didn't do their job, there would be no tomorrow. I had to get in touch with the gang. They needed to know what was at stake and I needed to know how everyone was doing. But most of all, I needed to contact Charlie. I had to tell her that Hali was coming for her!

Katarina Kreng turned her back and walked away from the webcam. She kept the link open though. I suppose she wanted to keep an eye on me. Swivelling around, I slyly put my Bluetooth earpiece in my ear. I dragged out my phone and dialled Charlie. It took a few seconds and then she smiled at me. She tilted her head to the side, a question in her eyes. I almost forgot why I had called. For a second I just stared.

'Hey Iago'

'Hey Charl''

'What's up?'

'Where are you?'

'Somewhere in the tunnel!' She panned the camera around so I could see. That brought back my focus!

'Listen Charlie, that weird guy – his name is Hali, by the way – he's been sent to find you. You are in danger. You really need to find the fail-safe and then get out!'

'OK Iago, I wish you were here with me…it's kind of, lonely…'

She dropped her head so I couldn't see her face. I felt so sad it hurt. But we had to be brave now. I had to make her feel strong. She couldn't cry out now!

'Charlie, this is really serious. This evil Kreng woman is going to annihilate the world because she believes she will be reborn on the other side. Probably thinks she'll be stardust or something stupid like that. We are the only ones who can stop her now. We're in this together but we all need to be strong!'

She took a deep breath and let it out slowly. And, looking straight at me, she smiled bravely, saying, 'Gotta go!'

'OK, seeya!'

And she was gone.

The real world swam back into focus. Funny, even when we were only talking over the phone, the rest of the world just faded into the background.

42
The Opening

Although I was worried about my Dad, I needed to call Renny next. I hadn't heard from either him or the girls for a while. I could be making all these plans and putting Charlie's life in danger for nothing. They needed to come through for me. Sometimes no news is good news, but not always. I was worried!

'Renny, tell me something…'

'Yeah, Iago, a little busy here at the moment. Could you be a bit more specific?'

'Sorry to be a bother Renny, but some of us are putting our lives in danger. Now DO you have an update for me!'

'OK, OK, the GST has reached out to as many kids as possible. They even posted on school intranet sites and library homepages. These guys are amazing...!'

'Renny!' I snapped.

'Anyway, the message is, for kids to switch on as many computers as they can. Kids are even walking into computer shops and logging on every computer in the shop. Once the computers are logged into 'The Grid', their hard drives are frozen and locked in. But even that much processing power won't be enough. The GST is trying to find us some extra juice. It means they will have to try to get into some big organisations, maybe electricity companies, banks, anyone with terabytes to spare! I don't know where you are with the countdown, Iago, but it will be tight!'

'It's got to happen Renny! There is no other way. You need to deliver!'

'Stop wasting my time then!'

* * *

I tried Cam next.

'Iago – perfect timing! We just got to the door.'

'The door of what – I thought you saw a flag?'

'Well the flag is on a pole in front of a huge metal door. It looks like a giant submarine hatch. It seems to be built into the side of the mountain.'

'What?'

'Mie says that it's an old bomb shelter. She says that there are dorms in some of them with bunk beds and kitchens and all. You can come and stay here on a school exchange trip. How cool is that?'

'Yeah Cam, that all sounds very cool, but well - things are not so cool here!'

'Oh, sorry Iago! We're going in…'

'What do you see?'

'Looking for the light-switch…OK, got it. I see one long corridor with lots of doors leading off.'

'Any message? Anywhere?'

'Not that I can see.'

'Just try all the doors then.'

'This could take a while!'

'You don't have a while!'

'Why…what do you mean?'

'If I heard right - Dad's on a train somewhere and…

There might be a bomb on that train!'

'WHAT? Why didn't you tell me Iago?

'Believe me - we've got an even bigger problem than that!'

'I'll find him Iago!'

'I know you will Cam! Call me when you find the clue!'

43
The Overlooked

I was getting frustrated. I could feel the adrenalin flooding my body now. I needed to be on the move. I needed to be doing something. But there was nothing for me to do. Then Tara called.

'Iago?'

'Hey Tar'! You OK?'

'Em…not really!'

'Go on!'

'Well the problem is… well Renny just called… and… well… you need to speak to him.'

'About what Tar'?'

'Well he says that someone needs to climb some building. Something about direct access to a server or something…Oh, I don't know Iago. Just call him! But I'll tell you one thing – I'm NOT climbing any buildings!'

'Nobody expects you to climb anything Tara. Just sit tight. I'll talk to Renny.

'Thanks Iago.'

'Bye Tar'.'

* * *

Angrily I punched Renny's number:

'Renny, what the hell's going on? Tara said you asked her to climb a building!'

'Well, someone's got to do it Iago! I'd do it but I have to stay here to coordinate things. Cam's off looking for your dad somewhere, so there's only Tara and Aretha left. I wasn't going to ask Aretha to do it, was I?'

'Back up a bit Renny. Why does anybody need to climb anything?'

'Oh yeah - sorry. Well I just heard from the GST. There's a problem… They can't get into the LHC's server. The last time they hacked CERN they only got into the CMS server.'

'What is CMS?' I interrupted.

'CMS is a detector – it's attached to the LHC but their control systems are separate. The computer that controls the LHC is physically separated from the mainframe.

'How do you mean - physically separated?'

'I mean - in another room, with no connecting wires or cables… completely "stand-alone."'

'But, why?'

They had to do this, so that nobody could hack in and start up the LHC from the outside.'

'But your dad needed THE GRID for his fail-safe to work. There must be a way to link to the LHC server!'

'Dad had direct access to everywhere at CERN. He could probably just walk up to the LHC server and plug in his laptop. I don't have that kind of access but I think I've found a way to build a bridge between the two systems.'

'What kind of bridge Renny?'

'Well… The LHC's server is on the top floor of the computer centre. There's NO way we can get into it from inside. So, I need someone to climb the outside of the building and get in through the roof. If Tara won't do it then it will have to be you. Once you're inside you will need to jack your mobile phone directly into the LHC's server. Then we can start transferring all the processing power from THE GRID. If everything works out as planned, we can power up Dad's fail-safe.'

'Renny, I hate to sound snippy but, WHY DIDN'T I KNOW ABOUT THIS BEFORE NOW?'

'Hey Iago... The GST didn't know exactly what we needed to do!'

'And whose fault is that Renny?'

'Hmmmphhh!'

'Sorry Renny, I didn't mean that – it's just that it's so last minute. I need to think! I'll call you back.'

'Later Iago!'

Renny was right - there was no one else who could do it – it had to be me. I needed to think of a way of escaping. But the witch was watching me!

That was it! She was watching me... All I had to do was make sure she kept on watching me!

I called Renny.

'Renny, you know earlier you fooled the security cameras to get Charlie through that door?'

'Yeah?'

'Well I need you to do it again! I've got to escape from here! This time I need you to loop the webcam feed so that Katarina Kreng sees me, even after I've gone. Can you do it?'

'It was easy to get in to the security cameras at CERN - dropping into a live webcam feed might be a bit above my pay-grade! ...but I think I know someone who might be able to help!'

'Who?'

'My friend on the inside!'

'You mean spottytechfreak!'

'Exactly!'

'Go for it Renny. Get back to me as soon as you know.'

'I'm on it!'

I breathed out a huge sigh. Now all I had to think about was the actual escape. I tugged my hands against the rope, hoping for some weakness. I wasn't going to be that lucky. Hali had tied the ropes tight and the knot looked secure. I was going to have to find some other way to free myself. And, without Katarina Kreng noticing!

My eyes scanned the room. There wasn't much in the room: apart from a small rucksack, that Hali had thrown on the floor by the desk. I had to check it out. There might be nothing in it to help me escape, but I had to try. Keeping my eyes on the screen, I began shuffling slowly forward. I had only moved about six inches forward when Katarina Kreng swung around. I froze instantly, my heart pounding. I tried desperately to keep still but my legs were starting to betray me. The effort of keeping them still was making the muscles jitter. Still, I stared straight at her as she stepped closer to the screen.

'Ah little gosling! You look so safe and snug there in your little nest. Do you know, you are so cute - I think I might take you with me!' She grinned and her huge teeth almost filled the screen. I winced, my stomach heaving. There was no way on this earth – or any other earth, for that matter – that I was going anywhere with that woman.

I couldn't let her know that though!

Although the thought of her made my skin creep, I decided to play along. I tried to look interested. Through clenched teeth, I smiled saying casually, 'How can you take me with you if you are somewhere else?'

'Oh don't worry, I'll be there shortly. I have to be there to deliver the final piece of my brilliant plan!' and giggling grossly, she held up a large metal canister to the camera.

'What is it?' I asked, although I felt sure I didn't want to know the answer.

'Well, let's just say it's insurance,' she replied. 'You see, the chance of creating a "killer strangelet" using the LHC is quite small. As you know, I must create "killer strangelets" if my plan is to work so, let's just say, I've upped the chances. During my time away from here, I found a way to super-charge my little protons.' She kissed the flask affectionately.

'There will definitely be "killer strangelets" once these babies are in the mix!'

She frowned slightly and looked into the camera, drawing her ugly mouth down in mock sadness. 'I'm afraid that you won't be able to see me for a little while. I have to get moving, but don't worry - I will still be able to see you! Don't miss me too much. I'll be with you very soon.' She blew a kiss into the camera and switched it off.

I almost retched with disgust.

Then Renny called.

44
The Old Camera Trick

'Iago, keep still. Remember the film "Speed"...no sudden movements. Spottytechfreak is ready to run the loop!'

'Renny, don't you know his real name?'

'Hmmm...never thought of asking!'

'Before we do this - can I just ask what your "handle" is? On second thoughts, I actually don't want to know. Just get on with it."

'OK, recording...'

'NOW!'

My phone's speakerphone was turned on. I had placed it on the floor and now remained absolutely still until I heard Renny giving me the all clear. I picked up my phone.

'Iago, we're running the loop... now'

'Thanks Renny, now I just have to figure out how to get out of here!'

'Can't help you with that, Cuz!'

'You just get back to what you were doing. Do you have enough juice yet?'

'I need to get back to the GST – see how they're doing. Call you back...'

I was free now to do what I could - which wasn't much since I was still tied to a heating duct. But I could shuffle forward and reach for the rucksack. Moving myself as far away from the heating duct as possible, I lay on my side and stretched my legs forward. My toe was just touching the strap of the rucksack. I tried to grip it with my shoe and tug it towards me but it didn't budge. It was just out of reach. I stretched out again and, breathing in deeply, I reached my foot forward one more time. Again, as I drew my foot towards me, the rucksack stayed exactly where it was. Breathing out a frustrated puff of air, I banged my head against the floor. I lay there for a moment, feeling hopeless. Then I remembered my dad…and Charlie…and Cam…and Renny…and Tara and Aretha. I took one more deep breath. I had to do this!

Stretching every muscle in my body, I folded myself along the floor like a snake. The rope around my wrists was pulled so tight that my hands were starting to go numb. I couldn't think about that now. Using every last millimetre of my body, I reached my foot forward. Slamming my foot against the strap of the rucksack, I kicked it backwards desperately. The rucksack flew back towards me - not very far, but far enough for me to reach it. Laughing with relief, I collapsed back on the floor.

The numbness in my hands didn't allow me to stay in that position for very long. Gripping the rucksack between my feet, I pulled myself back towards the radiator. As I did, the numbness was replaced by a painful tingling. I cried out in agony, as the blood rushed back into my fingers. Awkwardly, and with my hands still throbbing, I unzipped the rucksack.

Unable to use my hands properly, I tipped the contents of the rucksack on the floor in front of me. Dismay almost overwhelmed me as I saw that most of it seemed to be cables and other electronic bits and pieces. None of those was going to help me escape. Flipping the bag over, I fiddled with the zip of one of the side pockets. As I shook it, some USB pen-sticks rattled to the floor. They weren't going to help either. Desperately, I yanked open the zip to the other side pocket. I could feel that there was something heavy in there, so I shook the bag. The object wouldn't budge. I would have to squeeze my fingers into the small pocket and pull the object out. To my great relief it was a Swiss army knife.

Cutting through the rope took longer than I had hoped, but finally I was free. I didn't know how much time I had, but I needed to run. Stuffing the contents back into the rucksack, I swung it over my shoulder and bolted out of the door.

45

The Nerve

Knowing of no other way back to the main building, I was forced to go through the hatch and back into the rat-infested tunnel. This time I had no torch either. Deciding that it was best to just get this over with, I started to run. Maybe the rats would have gone somewhere else by now. Maybe if I were fast enough they wouldn't notice me. Maybe they were all asleep. I stumbled forward... hoping!

I didn't know if my eyes were playing tricks on me, but I thought I saw a glimmer of light up ahead. So intent on reaching the light, I forgot where I was, for just a split second. Then my right foot landed on something soft and the squeal that echoed through the tunnel was ear piercing. Jumping backwards in disgust, I held my breath, alert to every sound. I couldn't see it, but I knew that it was there. Suddenly, I felt something attacking my trouser leg. I shook it off. Guessing where the horrid creature was, I launched my foot at it. The sound of it hitting the tunnel further back was music to my ears.

'Gotcha!' I grinned. I didn't want to hang around too long though. I knew it had friends!

Launching myself at the metal ladder, I scurried up the first few rungs as fast as I could. I didn't know how high rats could climb, but I was pretty sure they couldn't make it up this ladder. At least I hoped they couldn't.

I reached the metal ledge that Hali and I had shared earlier. The hatch was still open. That was where the shaft of light came from. Carefully, I stuck my head through the hatch. Seeing no sign of anyone, I pulled myself through.

I needed to move fast so I yanked open the doors leading out of the maintenance shaft. Sprinting back down the corridor, I slammed through the emergency doors. My heart pounded as I raced back up several flights of stairs, my eyes scanning the signs by every door. Finally, I reached a door marked Ground Floor. There were lots of other signs indicating what could be found on the ground floor, but I was only interested in one thing - the WAY OUT sign!

I threw myself through the door. Several people standing in the corridor were surprised to see me sprinting past them. One lady even called out telling me to slow down. I was worried that someone might call security, so I smiled and slowed to a walk. Anxiously, I made my way out of the main building and looked around to get my bearings. Luckily, everything was signposted. Trying not to run, I followed the signs and soon I was looking up at the outside of the computer centre. Renny had made it all sound so easy but now that I was standing here facing it, I was terrified. The idea of shimmying up the side of a building is a lot easier than the reality!

Then my phone rang. I looked down angrily. I didn't have time to help anyone else right now. I barked a vicious 'Hello?'

'Iago, Cam here…'

'I haven't got time now, Cam…what is it?'

'Another clue...you want to hear it or not? I mean, it's your dad I'm trying to find...!'

'Yeah...go on...sorry!'

'"Where a journey takes you down a mount.

When gravity takes hold.

Oops, watch out. Don't spill a drop.

Or it might explode!"'

'Cam... we know this has something to do with a train and a bomb, but I have no idea where you need to go now, do you? Does Mie?'

'No. We're stumped!'

'OK, let me think for a while. You guys head for the train station. Maybe something will jump out at you when you get there...!'

'Good idea!'

'By the way Cam, where did you find the clue?'

'It was in the food storage area of the shelter. It was written on the side of a beer barrel.'

'Strange place to write a message...Anyway, I've got to go now Cam. Call me when you get to the station.'

'Later...'

I stared up at the building. Although I had scaled a few climbing walls in my time, this was truly frightening. I had no ropes and no buddy to watch my back. But, I reminded myself, the future of the world was in danger and so far nobody else had shown up to take over from me. As terrifying as it was, to admit, I didn't think anyone would.

Something about the beer barrel was ticking away in the back of my mind. I couldn't focus on that now though - I had to get moving! The white 1970's square block had plenty of ledges where I could rest, but the prefabricated concrete slabs would not have many handholds in them.

I continued around the building. Then I smiled. Luckily, the drainpipes and other systems were on the outside of the building in the old-fashioned style. I didn't really fancy it, but it shouldn't be too difficult to shimmy up from ledge to ledge. I just hoped that nobody would notice me.

Taking a couple of deep breaths, I started my climb. Very carefully, I wedged my foot between the drainpipe and the concrete wall behind it. Reaching for the edge of the first slab of concrete, I clamped my hands over it. I had to wiggle my foot free of the drainpipe so that I was hanging on by only my fingertips. Slowly, I dragged myself up, making a mental note to do more pull-ups before my next adventure. The muscles in my arms burned with the effort, but finally I could get my elbow over the ledge. After that, I just shuffled and dragged the rest of my body upwards, until all parts of me were safely on the edge of the first level.

One down... a few more to go! Then my phone rang again.

'Who is it now?' I groaned.

46
The Nub

'Iago...can you hear me?'
'Charlie...why are you whispering?'
'I heard a noise, somewhere behind me...Iago...I'm scared!'

'Charl' - I wish I could come and get you, but I've got to do something. You've got to be strong. There's no way that horrible creep can move as fast as you can. You'll find the fail-safe and be back to help me before he's done one kilometre.'

'Yeah...but the noise?'

'It's a giant tunnel with nothing in it. It's like a huge echo chamber. That sound could be miles away.'

'OK Iago... just wanted to hear your voice! Bye'

I had that strange pain in my chest again. I just wanted to fling myself to the ground and go protect Charlie. I really hated that Hali guy now. Anger swelled up inside me. If he hurt one hair on her head...

It took several deep breaths before I could open my eyes. I had to stay calm. The whole plan fell apart if I didn't get to the LHC server. Twisting my body around, I began my ascent of the second level. Although I was careful not to look down, in the back of my mind, I was aware of how high I was climbing. My arms were growing weaker each time I hauled myself up, and sweat was running into my eyes.

My mind began to wander as the monotony of dragging myself up by the fingertips took over. I was completely, in the zone. I was unaware of anything above or below me. I didn't notice any sounds. So the pigeon, flying in panic towards my head as I reached the ledge, startled me, to say the least. The bird, obviously used to his peace and quiet, was not expecting company. Seeing me as a predator, his self-defence mechanism kicked in, and, being a pigeon, he flew, stupidly, towards his attacker. Pigeons are possibly the most stupid of birds. Most birds would have gone in the opposite direction. His wing hit me full on in the forehead, the trailing feathers stinging my right eye. Fighting the urge to panic, I gripped tighter to the ledge, but the force of the bird's impact rocked me slightly and my right foot lost its grip. My body's equilibrium was upset now. My right leg dangling uselessly, all the weight now rested on the fingertips of my right hand. And, I could feel them sliding slowly back over the edge of the ledge. I had to act - I was too high up to fall now. I didn't allow myself to glance towards the ground - I knew that an impact from this height would mean certain death.

With an inner strength I didn't know I possessed, I pulled myself forward by the fingertips. Slowly, millimetre by millimetre, I dragged my body up. My right foot finally finding a firm footing, it catapulted my body the last few centimetres - almost as if it had a mind of its own.

Panting like a dog, I lay there on the ledge for what seemed like a very long time before I felt myself calm enough to consider going on. But, I had to - there was no one else to do this. So, with a lump of fear the size of a golf ball in my throat I carried on.

Reaching the edge of the final level, I dragged myself into a sitting position. Only then did I dare to look down. My eyes swam and my stomach lurched. I was really glad I hadn't looked down as I was climbing up. And, I was sure of one other thing; there was no way I was going back down the way I came up!

NO WAY!

With one final push, I swung my legs over the edge, onto the flat roof. Dragging my phone out I began to jog across the roof towards the emergency exit.

'Renny, where am I heading?'

'You there already?'

'Yeah!'

'Cool...! OK...what do you see?'

'Well...a door...obviously!'

'OK Iago, no need to be sarcastic! Is it locked?'

'Yep!'

'Wait...'

I waited, whistling impatiently!

'OK...try it now.'

Nervously, I turned the handle. To my surprise, it clicked open.

'I'm in. Where to next?'

Then my phone beeped, this time not due to an incoming call. My battery was about to die.

'Hang on,' I said as I disconnected the emergency charger from my belt. 'Thank Heavens for The Gadget Show!' That reminded me that I had promised to look after Charlie. She should have been with me, not alone and in danger.

'Renny!' I yelled sharply.

'I've got the schematic up, but I can't tell which way you are facing. You need to give me a marker,' He replied nervously.

'To my left the corridor goes on for a long way. I can see some signs at the end, but I can't read them from here. To my right the corridor bends sharply to the right after about ten metres. I can't see any signs there. Which way should I go?'

'Bear with me, just a second.'

'Renny…?'

'Patience, Iago. They didn't exactly draw an "X marks the spot" on the schematic. I am trying to figure it out.'

'Just give me a heading then. Time is ticking Renny!'

'Take the right, then…'

'You don't sound too convinced!'

'I'm not, but you're right - we have to try something.'

I raced around the bend to find another long corridor. Again, it was lined with doors on either side. All of the doors were numbered, but none was labelled. I sighed.

'Renny…I don't know how we are going to find the right room. There are no signs of any kind here… just numbers.'

'Iago…you fool! That's exactly what I need. The schematic has all the room numbers marked on it. They numbered the rooms before they labelled them. The builders didn't need to know what equipment was going where. They just needed to know that room 207 needed twenty electricity sockets and room 203 needed four air conditioners etc.'

'I didn't really need to know any of that Renny. And don't call me a fool again!'

'Sorry Man!'

'Which room number do I need, then?'

'Room 418.'

'Well, I'm standing in front of 435 right now. I'm just going to check the next number… its 437… and 436 is directly across the hall.'

'Ehem… Iago…I think you might need to go back the way you came.'

'You mean take the left not the right?'

'Um - yeah - sorry!'

'Call you back when I get there…'

I jammed the phone in my pocket and ran back in the opposite direction, checking the door numbers as I ran past them. 426…424…422…then my phone rang. Slowing to a walk, I pulled it out of my pocket.

'Cam?'

'We're at the train station and there's nothing much here,' he panted.

'Look around Cam. Tell me what you see!'

'I can see people getting onto the train that's in the station. We've already had a walk through it, and your dad's not on it. We've also checked the rest rooms and waiting rooms… Nothing!'

'There's got to be something Cam - a clue or something. And, whatever it is you've only got 15 minutes to find it. Look harder Cam, it's my dad we're talking about.'

'OK Iago… I can see that there's a train on the way down the mountain.'

'What…? How far down the mountain?'

'Still pretty close to the top. Why does that matter?'

Something started ticking in my head.

'Iago? Answer me,' yelled Cam. 'Why does it matter?'

My heartbeat slowed and fizzling lights appeared at the

edges of my vision. The corridor in front of me seemed to grow narrower. The ceiling and floor began moving towards each other. My mind froze, like a flower dipped in liquid nitrogen. Images panned left and right, like imprints behind my eyes. At first, they were random - railway engines with name plaques on the front, their shiny steam funnels glistening. Then, as if moving forward through history, the images changed from 1950's rolling stock, their many passenger doors swinging open, as commuters stepped down. Finally, I saw images of modern high-speed trains, hurtling cocooned passengers from the top of Europe to the bottom. All the while, one image remained fixed in the centre, right in front of my pupil - it was a nightmare vision of Katarina Kreng, a foaming bottle of beer in her hand. Although, like an ancient movie with no soundtrack, I couldn't hear her, I could see her mouth moving...

'Poufff!' she mouthed, throwing her head back, laughing wildly.

Suddenly, everything became crystal clear and I shouted, 'Cam - remember the beer barrel at the bomb shelter?'

'Yeah...?'

'And do you remember your dad telling us about the beer that goes flat if you take it down the mountain?'

'Yeah...?'

'Well... what if that mad witch rigged a bomb using the beer as a trigger?'

'Do you think that's even possible?'

'I don't know. I'm just guessing, but call Renny. He's bound to know. In the meantime, get on that train. If I'm right you need to get them to stop that train before it gets too far down the mountain.'

'OK Iago, I'm on it. Call you back.'

'OK, thanks Cam.'

Frozen in panic, I stood there gasping, reaching for the wall to steady myself. I had to pull myself together. I had to trust Cam to find my dad - I had something that I needed to do.

Taking a deep breath, I walked cautiously up to door number 418. I had no idea what was behind it. Would it be locked? Would there be security guards on the other side? Not really having time to worry, I tried the door handle. It turned silently in my hand.

'Bit easy!' I thought, but I carried on. Gingerly, I pushed the door open, just a crack. It was pretty dark inside the room with just a faint glow coming from the equipment. The only sound was the low hum of fans inside the computers, keeping their precious circuit boards at the right temperature.

Nobody shot at me or yanked the door open so I decided to go for it. If there was a security guard he was either asleep or had his back to me. Once the gap was big enough I stuck my head through - no one there! I slid inside the room closing the door carefully and stood with my back against it. My eyes started to grow accustomed to the dim light. Slowly, I began to make out shapes. Most of them appeared to be the usual grey box shapes I presumed were computers. I could see that they were in tall towers or racks. Deciding that I shouldn't risk turning on the lights, I crept forward carefully. I was almost on top of the racks before I could see that they were labelled. 'Very helpful,' I smiled to myself.

The only problem was - it was too dark to read the labels. Then I remembered that I still had Hali's rucksack on my back. I wiggled it off quietly and fumbled in it. It took a few seconds, but I did find a small torch right at the very bottom. I grinned - Good old Hali! Standing up, I started checking the rack labels. Most of them were just initials and meant nothing to me. Then I came to a few labels that started to mean something: CMS and Atlas. I knew that these were detectors attached to the LHC, so I was getting close.

Then Renny called.

47
The Nuts

'Iago?'

'Hey Renny – I found it. What do I need to do next? Just jack my phone and sit back and wait for you to build your bridge?'

'Oh, how I wish it were that simple.'

'What NOW Renny?'

'Well Tara and Aretha are in place. Aretha managed to distract one of the scientists, giving Tara the chance to connect her phone to the network. So, the good news is - we've got a signal going out of THE GRID! Aretha was brilliant, by the way. She's a born actress. She did the little girl interested in science gig sooo well. Tara says she's future Oscar material.'

'Yeah, I know she's a good actress – wonder where she got that from? But… what's the bad news Renny?'

'Well, assuming that Charlie does manage to locate the fail-safe AND switch it over, we still have one weak link – the mobile signal.'

'What's wrong with our mobile signal?'

'Well…'

'Renny. *What?*'

'Well…we've got nearly all the power we need going

into the GRID. Then we need to transfer ALL that power from Tara's mobile phone to your mobile phone.'

'Yeah Renny – I'm still with you. So where's the problem in that?'

'The problem is the bandwidth.'

'Remind me what bandwidth is, again?'

'Basically, it's the amount of space that your signal has out there, in the ether.'

'So - what's the problem with our bandwidth?'

'To put it simply – it's not big enough!'

'Why not?'

'Well, most mobile phone communications are pretty small so the satellite bandwidth doesn't need to be very large. Unfortunately, the quantity of data we need to transmit from Tara's phone to yours is… well… let's say… *huge!* If we try to squeeze too much data through a bandwidth that's too small, we could lose the signal completely.'

'Well…that DOES seem to be a problem Renny! Please let me know you're working on it!'

'Ah-hah old chap - when did I ever NOT have a plan?'

'What is it then?'

'Well – there's a satellite of which I know of!'

'Stop it with the Winnie-the-Pooh imitations Renny.'

'Sorry - couldn't help it! In any case, I think I might be able to find us a satellite with enough bandwidth.'

'Surely, there aren't satellites with massive bandwidths "just hanging around in space" that anyone can use? Renny - where exactly are you going to find this satellite?'

'Well… shhhhh – don't want to say this too loudly but have you heard of INTELSAT?'

'Kind of…'

'It's, sort of, operated by the military.'

'And, how on earth do you imagine you will be able to get control of it?'

'My "guys" can get in, but we might need a little help to turn the satellite the right way round – you know, so it's pointing in the right direction.'

'Are you calling the GST *my guys* now? Renny, you really are a berk!'

'Hey…who's working their fingers to the bone, trying to figure this out?'

'Sorry Renny! Oops – gotta go. Charlie's trying to get through. Call me back ASAP.'

* * *

'Charlie?'

…

'Charlie? I can't hear you. Please tell me you're alright...'

Nothing…

Kicking the wall in frustration, I decided to try Cam.

'Cam? Cam? Can you hear me now?'

'Yeah… just… about there…'

'Just about where, Cam?'

'…On the other train…'

'Which other train?'

'The one I hope your Dad's on… OK… we're on!'

'How did you make it?'

'We took the train heading up the mountain and when both trains stopped at a station; we jumped on the one heading down. It was pretty close though…'

'Can you see him yet?'

'There are a lot of people on here Iago… Oh, wait... Ohmigod…!'

'What is it Cam?'

'I see him... but he's definitely rigged with something. He... he seems to be unconscious.'

'Is he ALIVE?'

'Wait, I'm checking...'

'Please be alive Dad... Cam, for heavens sake... tell me!'

'I'm not a doctor Iago... wait... wait... I feel something... Yes, it's a pulse. He is alive Iago, but he looks like he's been drugged.'

'So he won't be able to help us. Cam, tell me what you see.'

'Well... his coat is slightly open and I can see - and I'm guessing here, what look like sticks of explosives. I don't see any ticking clock or anything, but I think you might be right about the beer.'

'Why?'

'Because, there's a bottle on the table in front of him. The lid of the bottle has been pierced and there's a tube running down into the beer...'

'Did you talk to Renny about the beer-bomb?'

'Yeah, but I didn't understand much of what he said.'

'OK Cam, do whatever you can to stop that train. I'll call Renny and get back to you...'

'Hurry Iago... Like I said – the train is pretty full.'

48
The No Choice

My heart pounded and the adrenaline burned as it snaked around my body. Shaking muscles hampered my efforts to keep calm. I had to do something. The constantly ringing phone was just making me more frustrated. As if reading my thoughts it beeped at me again. Swallowing a lump of frustration, I put it to my ear.

'Iago? Iago?'

'Yeah, I hear you Charlie!'

'I've found it!'

'Brilliant Charl' - but why are you whispering?'

'He must be really close behind me now. I'm sure I can smell him! Anyway, I'm going to arm the fail-safe…'

'Do you know what to do?'

'Kind of,' she replied. 'I just had a confusing conversation with Renny. You know how hard it is to work out what's important and what's just geek!'

I laughed in agreement. My cousin was brilliant and really useful, but you always had to listen with "Renny filters" on.

'So,' she continued. 'The fate of the universe relies on me working out how to arm this thing?!'

'If it makes you feel any better, there is one more job to

be done before we can consider the universe saved.'

'You mean - this isn't the end of our work?'

'Unfortunately not, but it doesn't make your job any less important. If you don't manage to arm the fail-safe then nothing else we do will matter, at all.'

'So - no pressure then,' she laughed, but I could hear the note of panic in her voice.

'I'll stay with you Charl',' I whispered.

'Thanks,' she replied softly.

'OK, here we go… I found the colour sequence that Renny got from his dad. He told me that the fail-safe mechanism should be inside the next junction box.'

'Have you found the junction box yet?'

'Gimme a minute,' she moaned.

'Sorry!'

'OK - I see it.'

I didn't dare say anything. I just waited patiently for her to open it. I think she appreciated my efforts, since she smiled at me. Reaching out her left hand, she gripped the cover of the junction box, tugging. A small squeaking sound drifted through her phone's mic, but the cover didn't budge.

Trying again, she swung all her body weight away from it, but still there was no movement.

'Have you got anything to jimmy it with?' I asked.

Then, I heard her rifling through her pockets.

'I've got a penknife,' she grinned.

'Good. Try to wedge it in somewhere.'

'I'll have to put you down,' she said, looking straight into the camera. 'But don't leave me. OK?'

It took me a second to work out what she meant. 'I'm not going anywhere,' I replied seriously.

With her phone on the floor, I had to rely on sound only. I could hear the scrape of metal on metal as she tried to lever the cover off. The next sound I heard was a loud metallic clang.

'Charlie - are you alright?' I shouted uselessly into the phone. She wouldn't be able to hear me anyway. "I" was on the floor - a long way from Charlie's ear. And besides, what could I do if it turned out that she wasn't all right?

Accompanied by shuffling sounds, the image of the ceiling began to shake - the phone was definitely moving.

'Hello? Hello?' I urged.

'Iago - are you there?'

Exhaling loudly I answered, 'Yes Charlie - I'm still here.'

'It came off,' she announced triumphantly. 'Hope they don't send us the bill. It's pretty trashed!'

'Do you see the fail-safe?'

'Um - it's not exactly marked, you know.'

'Did Renny have any idea what to look for?'

'He just said I'd know it when I saw it.'

'Very helpful of him.'

'Yeah - isn't he a treasure?'

I could hear the sarcasm in her last remark.

'Wait, this looks odd,' she said.

'Show me.'

The image of a small keypad came into focus as she held her phone steady in front of what she'd spotted.

'Yes - that's it,' I said, straining my eyes to see it in detail.

'Did Renny give you a password?'

'He just said to try names…'

'OK - try Renny first.'

'No - not that.'
'How about Cameron?'
'Nope!'
'Tara?'
'Not that either…'
'Try Meg…'
'Oh my God...!'
'Charlie?'
…
Charlie?'
…
'What was that noise? For heaven's sake Charlie, answer me… it sounded like a gunshot…'
…
'Ohmigod, Charlie - are you hurt?'
…
'Charlie?'
…
'CHARLIE?'
…
She was gone!

Fear struck me dumb. I just slithered down the wall and held my head in my hands. I'm not ashamed to admit that a tear welled in the corner of my eye. Images of Charlie flashed before me. Like stills, edited together to make a film, I saw her running, then smiling, then laughing, then crying. Anger boiled, bringing the fight back into my body. I would take matters into my own hands! Drawing air forcefully through my nostrils, I snatched my ringing phone.

'Renny, I just spoke to Cam. He's found Dad but, as we suspected, he's attached to some kind of beer-bomb. There doesn't seem to be any other trigger so tell me - how can beer trigger a bomb?'

'Well, I can't explain exactly, but it has something to do with the specific gravity of the beer. As the train heads down the mountain, the pressure increases. I think it makes the beer more dense but I'm not that sure. Look, all I know is that Cam needs to either get that beer back up the mountain, or somehow relieve the pressure in the bottle…'

'OK Renny, you need to tell him exactly that – no more, no less! And Renny…'

'Yeah?'

'Charlie's in trouble…! Whatever you need me to do, please tell me now so I can get out of here and go find her. Renny - I HAVE to help her!'

'OK, the GST can access Intelsat but someone needs to post a message on Youtube and Myspace and all the other sites.'

'Why haven't they done it yet?'

'Iago - they're hackers, for heaven's sake! They're hardly going to show their faces to the world. That would be the end of their careers and probably their freedom! No – you need to record the message and send it to me.'

'Why me?'

'Somehow, I don't think that many people will be moved by a message coming from ME. Do you?'

I couldn't really argue that one with him - he wasn't oozing with charisma. Renny was definitely a more behind the scenes guy.

'OK, OK – I'll record the message. Just tell me what they need to know.'

* * *

Charlie's number came up again. 'Oh thank you God!' I thought to myself, hitting answer.

I could see Charlie's face but she was a bit too far away. Something wasn't quite right.

'Charlie?'

…

'Charl', are you all right?'

'Hello, little gosling. Surprise!'

'Oh! I see you managed to escape! How bothersome! But don't worry - I'll send Hali back to find you. Isn't mobile phone GPS tracking fantastic? Oh by the way - is this your little girlfriend?'

'K.. K.. Katarina Kreng! What are you doing there?'

'Making sure there are no hiccups, my fluffy duck. You see, Hali forgot to tell me that your Uncle Jonas had a fail-safe. Well, he did remember actually, but only after I sent him to find your little fluffy friend here. He is such a fool. He couldn't shoot straight in a straight tunnel, so there was no chance of him hitting a moving target down here! That gunshot you heard ricocheted off the tunnel wall five times before it stopped. Your girlfriend is a very lucky little ducky.'

She gazed off into the distance before returning her attention to me. 'But, sadly for her, her luck has just run out. Now she'll be the first to find out what it's like to slip over the edge of a black hole. In one way I envy her – you see, she will get to see it "up close and personal", whereas you and I will only see it through the window!'

'The window of what?'

'Oh now you've upset me, my darling. You didn't think I was crazy – did you? The window of the craft I've spent the last seven years working on. I know that all matter will be annihilated after the event, so I've built a small pod with an anti-matter shield. And! Best of all - it's big enough for two! It'll be a bit tight, of course, but I don't mind. Do you?'

'Uuuggghhh…' I spat, clenching my fists. This witch was really getting under my skin.

'So, anyway… your little girlfriend tells me she has managed to arm the fail-safe. I should be quite annoyed with her. But I'm not! Well I am just a teeny bit annoyed, so I thought I'd tie her to the fail-safe mechanism. What poetic justice – she vaporises along with the fail-safe she searched so hard to find!'

'Let her go, you horrible witch!'

'Temper, temper - my golden goose! We will have to work on that, when we're together!'

'Your stupid plan will never work, not now the fail-safe has been switched on!'

'Oh - but, it will. You see Hali just explained that your Uncle needed to connect THE GRID to the LHC server directly to activate the "fail-safe" once it had been armed. And… well, last I heard… He's in custody. So unless, you little gooses could - I don't know… put your fluffy little heads together and find a cable long enough to connect them… Well, let's just say that the fail-safe doesn't really figure in my plans right now.'

'Put Charlie on…'

'Oh, is that her name? Do you know, I forgot to ask you your name. How forgetful of me! Imagine not knowing the name of the person you are going to spend the rest of your life with. Oh dear, I must be getting old! Tell me your name and I'll let you say goodbye to your pretty girlyfriend!'

My voice caught in my throat, like a half-eaten

gobstopper. I knew I had no choice. I had to answer her.

'My name is …Iago and…'

'And what - my beautiful boy?'

'And… I'll go… with you. But, only if you let Charlie go now.'

'Hmmmm… interesting offer! I'll tell you what – I'll bring your little ducky with me as an insurance policy. If you meet me at the pod, I will let her go!'

'Ok, where and when?'

'Oh… let me just check my countdown… hmmmn… meet me in twenty minutes at the Atlas detector. Be there or be - well, you know… vaporised!'

That did it. I was not going to sit around anymore and wait for Renny's geeksquad to give me the message. Jacking my phone into the LHC server, I stuck my Bluetooth earpiece in, and ran for the door. If Tara called while I was gone, I'd still be able to pick-up. In the meantime, I was going to get to Charlie. I had no idea of what I could do to help but anything was better than nothing!

49
The Never Ever

Springing past the computer towers, I made my way to the door. I turned the handle slowly, making just enough of a gap for one eye to peep through. There didn't seem to be any activity in the corridor outside so I swung the door fully open. As my left foot stretched over the threshold, something exploded just above my head.

'God No! Not again!' I screamed silently, bolting back inside the computer room. I knew who it was - it could only be Hali. No security guard, in their right mind, would shoot first and ask questions later.

Anger bubbled so close to the surface now that I could hear it boiling in my ears. I had only twenty minutes to save Charlie and try to stop the annihilation of everything we knew, and this stinking trigger-happy misfit was back to haunt me.

After taking several long slow breaths to calm myself, I slunk behind one of the computer racks. I could see the door through a gap between two machines. I had one major advantage - there were at least twenty of these stacks in the room - Hali would have to figure out which one of them I was behind.

He blasted through the door in his usual style. Subtlety

was not high on his list, along with dental hygiene and manners! My eyes actually stung as he entered the stuffy, sealed room. He shifted from one foot to the other, swinging his gun from left to right – FBI style. I might have laughed at his comic image, had it not been for the fact that death would have been… well… just a shot away… Again, some of Dad's music floated into my mind - 'War…children… it's just a shot away… it's just a shot away.' The smile that was forming on my face froze. There would be no children to sing to, if I didn't pull my finger out.

Without thinking, I sprung out of my hiding place and made a dash for the door. Sparks flickered all around me as Hali shot wildly, his shots pinging off bits of metal racks and computer hardware. I dived for the cover of a wooden desk, which I upended just in time to stop Hali's next trail of shots. Not knowing much about guns, I worried that I might be killed if I stayed where I was. Then I heard a click, click sound, and Hali swore. I couldn't be sure, but it sounded to me like he had run out of bullets. This was my chance.

Standing up squarely from behind the desk, I grinned at Hali.

The grin quickly changed to an upside-down-smile as I saw Hali pull something out of his pocket. It looked very much like another gun clip.

Yup - it was! Hali casually clipped it into the bottom of the gun.

Like a startled deer, I bounced at least three feet into the air before diving for cover behind another of the computer towers. As I lay there, flat on my belly, I realised that if Hali managed to somehow hit the LHC server, our entire plan was down the toilet. I had to draw him out of here, or stop him somehow.

'Hah… you little fool. You can't get out of here, you know!' he tittered, tilting his head back. 'By the way, I thought your little girlfriend was quite the prettiest thing I've seen for a while. Who knows, maybe when I am one of the richest men in the world she could force herself to love me. Money and power make men attractive to females, you know!'

He'd finally done it. Not only was he totally insane, but now he'd managed to make me feel like vomiting. To even mention Charlie in that way was the straw that broke the camel's back. From somewhere, deep down inside me a power erupted.

In one move I was standing, leaning against the computer tower in front of me. My second move saw me halfway up it, and less than a second later, I was clinging to a metal roof-beam, pushing with my legs against the rack. A small squeak was all that Hali heard before the rack came toppling towards him. In his surprise, he reached his arm up and shot at the rack, as if that were his attacker. Swinging my legs like a dismounting gymnast, I flung myself to the side, away from his searching bullets.

'Ouch!' I groaned aloud, as I landed with a thud on the concrete floor. I knew I didn't have time to nurse my injuries. I had to make sure that Hali was no longer a threat. There was so much riding on me getting out of here. I began to worry that everyone else would be left sitting there, having done their part, waiting while Katarina Kreng's wicked plan was realised. A wave of negativity washed over me and I almost wallowed in defeat. Banging my fist on the side of my head, I shouted at myself, 'C'mon man!'

Shifting sideways, ape-like, to the fallen tower, I peered

round it. Hali's hand was sticking out the side of the metal rack, reminding me of Dorothy's house falling on the wicked witch of the west in The Wizard of Oz. The gun lay just beyond his fingers. Quickly kicking it away, I crept towards the top of the fallen tower. I felt a strange mixture of emotions. I felt overjoyed that Hali was no longer a threat to me but at the same time terrified that I might have actually killed him. My head swam as I bent down to check his pulse.

As my fingers touched his neck a scream erupted from his mouth, 'don't touch me you vile little creature! You will be sorry when I get hold of you. The whole operation is in Katarina's hands now and once she has achieved our goal, she will come and find me. There is nothing you can do now…you…pipsqueak!' As he lay there trapped, I almost felt sorry for the horrid pathetic little man. But that lasted only a heartbeat.

Bending my head as near to him as I could bear, I smiled sweetly as I said, 'She will not be coming for you Hali. How stupid are you? Could you not see that she was insane? Your greed blinded you from seeing the truth - you were a means to an end. This is bigger than your nasty little bid for power and wealth. Katarina Kreng has much, much bigger plans!'

I paused, waiting to see whether he understood. The Jekyll and Hyde within him fought each other, as he tried to comprehend what I was telling him. His face altered between that of a grinning idiot and a whimpering child. He simply couldn't compute what I was saying.

Anger drove me towards him. Grabbing his collar, I shook him roughly, shrieking, 'She has built an anti-matter pod - you idiot! She isn't going to stop on the brink of annihilation… she's going all the way. She is going to annihilate the world!'

I watched as the colour drained from his face and his skin started to take on a greenish hue. He mumbled something to himself as I stood up. I didn't care about him anymore. He was clearly mentally unstable. Something in his life had tipped him over the edge, but that was still no excuse for his actions. As I reached the door, I couldn't help but turn back and say, 'We are all that stands between you and oblivion, so you'd better hope we can stop this in time…'

Turning angrily, I burst through the door.

50
The Necessary

Hey guys! I'm interrupting myself to tell you that everything has changed. I'm going to have to leave you stuck here. Hopefully, just for a while. Um... if, in the sands of time, anyone, anywhere, in any universe, ever finds this message and it ends here, then I guess I messed up. But well, as you might have guessed - Charlie means quite a lot to me. And sometimes you have to go with your heart, not just your head.

51

The Now and Forever

No matter what else happened I needed to get to the Atlas detector. If I didn't make it there and back in the next fifteen minutes... No, I didn't even want to think about that possibility.

Try to stay positive, Iago,' I told myself. 'Just focus on rescuing Charlie, for now!' I found myself smiling foolishly, as I thought of Charlie. Oh no! Now I was annoying myself. Just keep focused, you idiot.

I turned my head frantically from left to right, trying to think. There was no way I was going out the way I came in. Or rather, down the way I came up! Though, the idea of being chased around by security guards didn't exactly light my fire either. I was about to call Renny to ask for help in avoiding them, but then decided not to. Time was ticking.

Throwing caution to the wind, I legged it down the corridor to where I'd seen the signs earlier. Sprinting flat out, I followed the signs to the emergency exit. I slammed through the doors, not caring what alarms went off. To my surprise, there were no bells or beeping sounds, so I jumped the steps three at a time. By the time I reached ground floor level, I was almost flying down the stairs.

Luckily, I hadn't put a foot wrong. The image of myself in a mangled heap at the bottom of a stairwell flashed before my eyes. This time I laughed it off. I wasn't going to listen to any doubting voices anymore. I felt strangely stronger. I felt somehow, more mature.

Bracing myself, I bounced against the exit door. It flew open and I landed outside on the concrete pavement, quite hard. Pulling myself up painfully, I scanned the buildings to try to work out my location. It was no use – I'd have to call Renny. Hitting the dial-out button on my earpiece, I voice-dialled Renny's number, jogging forward slowly.

'Renny…'

'Where are you? Are you running? You are supposed to be recording the video file for me and more importantly – you're supposed to be by the LHC server so we can set up the bandwidth bridge!'

'Don't worry Renny. I've got my Bluetooth earpiece. I can still pick-up when Tara calls.'

'Um… Iago, I hate to rain on your parade but the Bluetooth has a limited range. You need to be within 100 metres of your phone to answer it. You should have called me before you left your post.'

'Well…I'm not going back there now Renny. You can court-martial me captain! Look - I'm just going to get Charlie and then hightail it back there. I promise I won't let you down. I'll be back in time for THE call. I promise!'

'Iago, you've got less than fifteen minutes. It took Charlie longer than that just to get to the fail-safe. You'll never make it back…!'

'I'm not meeting them at the fail-safe. I've got to get to the Atlas detector.'

'Iago, who are "them" and why do you need to go to the

Atlas detector?'

'Renny, Katarina Kreng has Charlie and I said I would meet her by her ship.'

'Ship? Iago, what do you mean *ship?*'

'Oh sorry, I forgot to tell you. That mad witch has built some kind of anti-matter ship and intends to travel through the black hole.'

'Cooool! ...oh sorry man. Annihilating the world would definitely not be cool. But, travelling through a black hole... Wow - just imagine!'

'Renny...back to reality. I need directions. You need to get me to Atlas and back in the shortest time possible.'

'OK. Where are you now?'

'At the back exit of the computer centre.'

'OK you need to follow route Rutherford, then route Einstein until you get to the main road. You should be able to see the Globe centre from there. I'll work on getting you into "point 1," which is the closest entry point to Atlas. By the way, did you know that you are actually in France, at the moment?'

'Gripping stuff Renny, but I've got to run.'

With my legs pumping harder than they ever had before, I reached the corner and turned up route Einstein. I scarcely had time to think about the brilliant scientists these streets were named after.

A little further up I could just make out the top of the huge Globe centre to my left. Dashing around the corner, I nearly flattened some poor man carrying arms full of files. In his surprise, he dropped some of them on the ground. 'Sorry...!' I shouted back over my shoulder. I really was sorry, but I didn't have the time to help him pick them up.

Dodging a bus, I flung myself across route de Meyrin

and dashed towards the Globe centre. Slowing to walking pace, I searched for "Point 1" as Renny had mentioned. As soon as I got to the door, I voice dialled Renny again. My Bluetooth earpiece seemed to have a decent range because he picked up.

'You there already?'

'Yeah!'

'I don't even think Charlie could have done it in… let me check… two minutes ten seconds!'

'Renny - tell me you can get me in.'

'Listen Iago, I am not about to fail now.'

'Thanks Cuz, you may be off your rocker, but I can always rely on you.'

'Reliable Renny, they call me!'

'Is that your geekname? No, don't tell me yet. Tell me when this is all over.'

'You betcha!'

'Geek!'

'And proud of it!'

52
The Nemesis

Once inside the door, it seemed that I was pretty much on my own. I didn't have time to waste, so I couldn't dither. Choosing the left corridor, I jogged silently past several doors. I couldn't tell what was in the rooms I passed, but from the spacing of the doors, they must have been offices. Katarina Kreng's anti-matter pod couldn't be in any of these rooms – they weren't exactly private. Somehow, I couldn't imagine her hauling her pod down the corridor and parking it in someone's office.

Picking up the pace, I headed for the double doors at the end of the corridor. As I got nearer, I could make out the signs above the doors. There were three blue signs, but it was the one in green that interested me most - it read: Atlas Lab.

Following the green arrows, I sprinted and swerved my way down another long corridor until I came to a door marked Atlas Laboratory. Peeping through the small window in the top of the door, I could see that this was a huge space. The giant hunks of shining metal spread around the lab suggested that the technicians brought bits of the huge detector here to reset or cleaned or something. There didn't seem to be anyone in, so I slipped carefully inside.

With only the central lights on, my eyes strained to make out the far end of the lab. Sensing rather than seeing movement, I instinctively crouched down, making myself as short as possible. Also, realising that I was in the most well lit part of the room, I crawled along the wall until I found some shadows into which I could disappear.

A sudden rattle from somewhere in the darkness made my right ear shoot up. My head swivelled on instinct and my eyes searched. Now I understood why Man slept at night. Our species would have been wiped out in the blink of an eye, if we had tried to hunt after sunset. Of course, there's probably some geneticist working on that as we speak. Imagine that – designer babies with night vision!

Blurry images moving against a still backdrop was all that my light-starved eyes could make out. And if I blinked too hard, even these images disappeared. Losing patience with my inadequate DNA, I headed towards the moving images. Then a light suddenly flickered to life. Like a rabbit in the headlights, I froze mid-step. My startled mind caught up with reality, just in time for me to duck down behind a giant metal fitting.

Peering around the side, I could see them both. My heart pounded. There was Charlie, hands tied behind her back, with a gag over her mouth. She seemed to be attached to a huge metal ring, and scattered all around her were bits of piping and what must have been component parts of the LHC, or one of its detectors.

Seeing that Katarina Kreng was walking away from me, I jumped up to get Charlie's attention. The ticking countdown on Katarina Kreng's laptop almost outweighed the joy I felt as Charlie smiled. Well it was hard to tell if she was smiling because of the gag, but she looked happy to see me.

Unaware of my presence, Katarina Kreng headed towards a large metal sphere near the back wall of the lab. Taking a deep breath, I ran as fast as I could towards Charlie. Her eyes flashed angrily at me, as I got nearer. What was she angry about? I was coming to rescue her!

Then everything came crashing down around me as Katarina Kreng turned to face me. The shock in her face showed that she hadn't been expecting me quite so soon.

'Ah - my goosey goosey gander! Come over here and wonder at my lady's chamber.' She guffawed at her own joke, pointing to the sphere.

I took a step closer to Charlie. 'So, you'd rather die along with your little friend than live a lifetime amongst the stars,' hissed the madwoman. The tone of her voice made my blood curdle.

'I'd rather have one minute with Charlie than a million years with you,' I hissed.

'You may have your wish then!' she spat as she unexpectedly flew in my direction. Stunned by her sudden movement, I almost didn't respond. Then Charlie's muffled voice woke me up and I ran towards her. Knowing that Katarina Kreng would be on me in a second, I grabbed a length of pipe from the scattered debris on the floor and swung it behind me, catching the witch on the ankles. For a fleeting second I felt bad about causing pain to someone else, then reality kicked in - if I didn't stop her, she would end the world.

As she stumbled past me, I pulled Hali's Swiss army knife out of my pocket. The sharp blade sliced through Charlie's ropes and I grabbed her hand to pull her forward.

'Feet!' she screamed, tearing the gag from her mouth.

In slow motion, I followed her eyes. The penny only dropped when I noticed the rope around her ankles! 'Idiot,' I swore at myself, under my breath. Bending to cut the rope, I hadn't noticed Katarina Kreng staggering to her feet behind me.

With the squeal of a wild cat, she sprung onto my back. The hairs on my neck stood up in protest. With a strength I didn't know that I possessed, I pushed myself off the floor and stood up. Her horrible fingers scratched at my face as her legs wrapped around my waist. I could feel the warm trickle of blood flowing from one of the scratches. Realising that the witch was going for my eyes, I squeezed them shut. This made fighting her a lot harder. I staggered backwards as she alternately pulled at my hair and poked at my eyes.

Then her tactic changed. Like a vice, she locked her hands around my neck and started to squeeze. My hands flew to my neck, trying to prise hers off. Her grip was strong. My vision started to blur as a loud pounding noise echoed around my head. My oxygen-starved brain was having trouble working out what was happening. My limbs were growing weaker. I felt like I was falling. The last sound I heard was a dull "clunk."

53
The Nefarious

Objects swam back into focus and my neck started to tingle as blood flowed through my veins once again. The most amazing object of all though, was Charlie's smiling face. Amazing... because it was the last thing I expected to see.

'What happened?' I groaned, dragging myself up off the floor.

'Well! I hit her with this,' Charlie grinned, holding up Katarina Kreng's "super-charged protons" flask.

'Sweet irony,' I replied, looking down at the wicked witch.

'Shame she got the chance to empty it first,' said Charlie wistfully, pulling me forward. I wobbled slightly and she had to steady me. Instinctively I rested my arm on her shoulder. She circled her arm around my body. I think it was for support, but she held me just a little bit tighter than she needed to.

Looking down at her face, I felt happy. As she smiled back at me, I noticed how dark her pupils were. A pang of something hit me in the chest and I lowered my head towards her. My Bluetooth signal screaming in my ear completely annihilated that moment.

'Iago?'

'Renny - I thought you said that my Bluetooth had a limited range?'

'Yeah it does! But I managed to isolate your signal and amplify it.'

'Renny, you may be a nerd but you are also a genius.'

'Yeah I know, I know! And I know that you're busy but have you noticed how long we've got left?'

I turned my face towards the laptop screen. Charlie's gaze followed mine. Before she could scream, I grabbed her arm and started pulling her towards the door. 'What about her?' Charlie shouted, looking back towards the crumpled heap on the floor. Running over to where she lay, I grabbed her under the shoulders. Charlie followed my lead, grabbing her ankles. Awkwardly, we dragged her to her precious pod. The door was open so I backed in, dragging her inside. The hideous creature was heavier than expected and I stumbled over the doorframe, falling backwards. Her deadweight landed right on top of me, pinning me down. The look of horror in Charlie's eyes must have been mirrored in my own as I struggled to free myself. I couldn't be trapped by Katarina Kreng's unconscious body - that would just be too cruel. Shifting my weight to one side, I tried to slide my leg out from under her. If I could just release it far enough to bend it, I could lever her off.

'Charlie - help me. Grab her wrists!' I cried.

Wrinkling her nose in disgust Charlie reached out gingerly, taking her wrists reluctantly - as is she were holding two deadly snakes.

'Pull,' I shouted.

Then Charlie screamed - a blood-curdling scream of

pure terror.

At first, I couldn't work out why she was screaming, but then the witch's bodyweight shifted on top of me and I knew she was awake. Now, instead of Charlie holding her wrists, Katarina Kreng grabbed Charlie's pulling her to her knees. With her full bodyweight still on me, I remained trapped.

'How perfectly lovely,' she said, twisting her ugly head back towards mine. My stomach heaved in revulsion.

'But I don't want your little girlfriend spoiling our fun.' With that, she shoved Charlie backwards forcefully. As I watched Charlie tumble out the doorway, I felt Katarina Kreng's weight shift slightly, releasing my upper body. I had only a split second to act! Groping around above my head, I picked up the first object my hand encountered - I hoped it was something hard! With all the force I could muster from that position, I swung the object forward, hitting her square on the top of her head. Luckily for me, it had been a plastic food box, crammed full. She wasn't unconscious, just stunned. But she was stunned just long enough for me to free myself. Shoving her body aside, I sprang to my feet, leaping for the door. Charlie, having recovered from her hard landing, slammed the door closed, as I dove through. Then, using the long metal rod I'd thrown on the floor earlier, I jammed the lock. She wasn't getting out of there in a hurry.

* * *

'Renny…you still there?'
'Yeah…'
'Get security down here. Tell them the wicked witch of the west is not quite dead, but at least she's trapped…

'...for now.'

54
The Never Give Up

Grabbing Katarina Kreng's laptop in one hand, I reached out for Charlie with the other. She took my hand gently and I felt something like happiness. Then sadness. Then pain and horror, as I thought of the world ending and never seeing Charlie or anyone else again.

She shrieked as I pulled her forward so violently that I almost took her arm off.

'Sorry!' I winced as she looked at me crossly. 'Really cool Iago!' I said to myself. Why, when things seemed to be going well between us, did I always find a way to mess it up? Must be some unique talent I was born with. Wonder if any other lucky person on this earth shares my gift?

She laughed at me and started running. Remember I said that she was a fast runner. Well, she's not just fast; she's incredibly fast. Within seconds, I was left well behind. Her long dark hair swirled around her face as she turned back to check on my progress.

'Iago - move it!' she shouted.

'Kind of… carrying stuff,' I shouted back, in my own defence. She stopped and when I caught up, she grabbed the laptop. She couldn't resist opening it just a little. The look on her face stopped me from asking a stupid question.

I knew we didn't have much time. This time I ran!

Retracing my steps from memory, I headed towards the exit point.

'Five minutes!' shouted Charlie from just behind my shoulder. We burst through the doors and I took the lead. Remembering how long it had taken me to run down the roads named after famous scientists sent a shiver down my spine. Charlie seemed to read the fear in my face when she caught up with me because her smile of triumph at having caught me quickly vanished. We both put our heads down and sprinted towards the computer centre's emergency exit.

'Renny…the door…,' I screamed as we reached it.

'One step ahead…' he screamed back. Renny, the unflappable, was sounding just a bit on edge.

The doors imploded as Charlie and I flung ourselves at them. Taking the emergency stairs three steps at a time, we started towards the top floor. Taking the lift may have been faster, but I doubted we would have been able to stand still and wait for it to come. The adrenaline was in full flow now and our muscles were warmed up like springs. Now I really understood our hidden animal instincts. The fight or flight instinct is there in all of us. It's a survival mechanism that drives us forward, even if what we face seems impossible.

We didn't have time to check the countdown again as we barrelled along the corridor towards the LHC server room. 'Which room?' rasped Charlie. I was glad to know that even she was starting to feel the effects of our flat-out sprint. It was all I could do to point towards the door - I didn't trust my voice not to crack. 'Legs – don't fail me now!' my brain urged as I bounced against the door.

Leaping over the fallen computer tower, I raced to my phone. Hali moaned as I passed him and Charlie threw him such a look that he whimpered and turned his head away.

'Renny!' I screamed

'What the hell is this message I need to transmit. I've got to do it now if anyone's going to respond in time!'

'I'm streaming you live. The message you need to send is on the bottom of your screen… Hurry up Iago!'

55
The Need You Now

Huh... huh... huh... sorry guys. I just need to catch my breath. Huh... huh...

So... Renny can turn the satellite around but he needs your help...

Now it's ALL up to you. You need to do this and you need to do it NOW!

The coordinates for CERN are La431359N/Lo6320E.

Log on to www.arctic6.com and enter the text. Renny will take care of the rest.

If you can't get online - text the coordinates to 20100331.

After you've done it please, please pass the message on to everyone you know......

Please I'm begging...

For all of us...

DO IT RIGHT NOW !!!!!!!!!
...
...
………………………………Charlie...
Hold my hand?

Epilogue

It was touch and go for a couple of minutes and to be honest, I didn't know if I could count on you. But... well... we're still here!

And my Dad – yes, he's still here too. It's quite funny how Cam solved the beer-bomb problem in the end. Using just a tiny bit of science, he figured that if the pressure inside the bottle was going up as the train went down the simplest way to lower the pressure was to... drink the beer. He managed to slide a straw down inside the bottle and suck out about half of the beer. Luckily, for him, the police understood the situation and didn't charge him with underage drinking. He did have a headache and an awful dry mouth afterwards. But, since Mie was there to massage his head, I think he didn't really mind. As you can imagine, he's hoping not to have to deal with any more beer bombs in the near future.

As for the rest of us? Well, the scientists, not surprisingly, want to keep this whole thing hush-hush. A bit difficult, given the fact that I had to broadcast live on every net page I could to get your help. But, you know... adults... they can ignore a lot. If it isn't on the six o'clock news, then it didn't happen. Which, in one way, is good. I mean – if they don't really understand how we communicate, then at least we have some privacy. We can share ideas globally, maybe come up with better solutions to global problems. You know… they're not tackling global warming and they probably never will. They strip the land to grow crops we don't need. They do nothing about trying to redistribute food to people who do need it. They just keep on using up all our reserves of oil and minerals. They say they are interested in renewable energy, but I don't think they're trying hard enough. Just imagine how much energy Africa could produce if someone installed Solar Cells across the Sahara..!

So, at the very least… keep talking to each other. Someday, we will be in charge.

Then WE can make a change!

Oh… and, don't forget to check out *arctic6blog*… every now and then!

You never know what might happen!

Coming Soon...

Look out for the next

arctic⁶

adventure!

www.arctic6.com

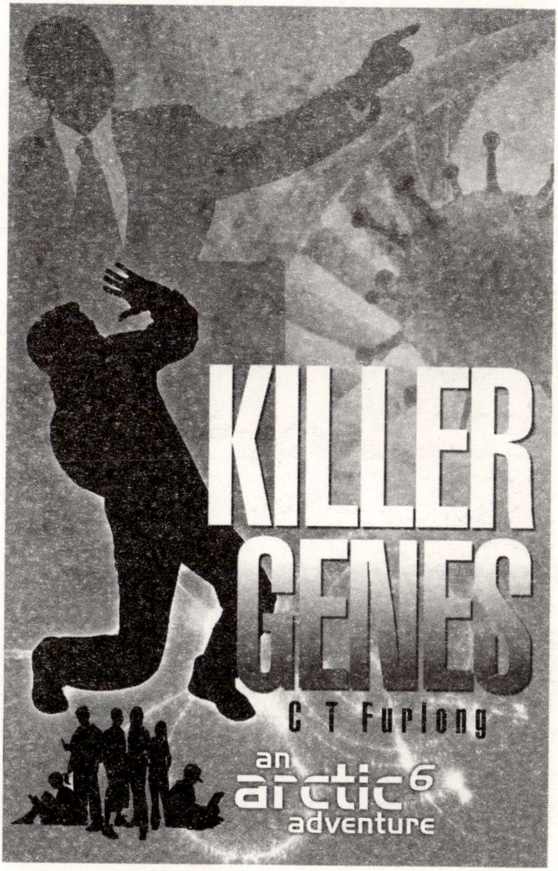
KILLER
GENES
C T Furlong
an
arctic6
adventure